M

# Untold Tales

# Untold Tales

by

## William J. Brooke

HarperCollins*Publishers*

Typography by Daniel C. O'Leary
1   2   3   4   5   6   7   8   9   10
First Edition

Library of Congress Cataloging-in-Publication Data
Brooke, William J.
   Untold tales / William J. Brooke.
      p.      cm.
   Summary: Retells and continues the stories, from a contemporary perspec-
tive, of classic tales such as "The Frog Prince," "Snow White," "Beauty and the
Beast," and "Sleeping Beauty."
   ISBN 0-06-020271-8. — ISBN 0-06-020272-6 (lib. bdg.)
   1. Fairy tales—United States.   2. Children's stories, American.   [1.Fairy
tales.]   I. Title.
PZ8.B682Un   1992                                        91-4179
[Fic]—dc20                                                  CIP
                                                              AC

With love to My Parents
Who gave me a good first draft
and to Lynne
My Co-Author

# Contents

A

*P*rince

*in the*

*T*hroat

*O*nce upon a time, there was a Frog Prince.

The Princess felt sure there was more to him than just amiable green ugliness. For example, he treated her as if she were the most important thing in the world, and that was certainly an attractive quality.

He was very attentive to her and always spoke in verse. She would close her eyes and imagine him as a handsome Prince. Sometimes in her imagination he was blond, then again dark; now willowy, now muscular; now poetic, now courageous in battle. All her imaginings were so wonderful that she finally just squinted her eyes to blur what he *really* looked like and gave him a kiss.

Immediately, there sprang up the very most

handsome Prince she could ever have imagined, although not precisely any of the ones she *had* imagined. He wed her and carried her off to meet his father, and eventually they became the King and Queen of his homeland. And they lived happily ever after.

But now and then, there hopped into her mind all those other Princes that he wasn't.

✤    ✤    ✤

*O*n *the occasion of her forty-fifth birthday,* all the kingdom gathered to honor the Queen. There were parades, tourneys, a grand marketplace, and general rejoicings. The highlight of the evening was the great banquet, which was spread from the castle drawbridge down through the main street of the town to the great gate of the kingdom. Everyone was invited, and all brought candles to the feast. From the balcony where the King and Queen sat above the moat, a river of light flowed down the hillside as far as the eye could see.

After the various lords and nobles had offered their gifts and personal best wishes, it was time for the toast to the Queen. All raised jeweled goblets or pewter tankards or pottery mugs, according to their various stations, and stood as the King cleared his throat.

The King was nervous. He was very used to public speaking and normally quite eloquent, but there was something about expressing his feelings for the Queen that tied his tongue. So he glanced surreptitiously at a text that had been prepared for him by the Lord Chamberlain. "On this joyous occasion," he began tentatively, "I must address you as 'My fellow subjects,' since I, too, am merely a vassal to the true ruler of all our hearts."

As the throng roared its approval, he glanced at the Queen. She was staring off into space, as if listening to some other voice entirely. The King fixed his eyes on the parchment and hurried on. "So I join with all of you in lifting a toast to my radiant Queen." He lowered his notes. "The dearest one I've ever seen," he added, gazing at her sadly.

She seemed to hear something then. Her head lifted and her eyes suddenly lit up as she swung about to face him. "That was a poem!" she gasped in pleased astonishment.

"What? No, it wasn't," he replied, startled.

"It rhymed, it had meter . . ."

"I don't think so," the King said quickly, trying to

find his place in the notes.

"'De dum, de dum, de dum de Queen/The dearest one I've ever seen,'" the Queen repeated happily in a sing-song voice.

"It was an accident, I assure you," the King said defensively. "One of those things that sneaks in when you aren't careful about what you're saying."

The Queen's eyes clouded over. "I thought you made a rhyme for me."

All the people were staring in bewilderment. "I have no gift for poetry," the King said, embarrassed.

"There! That was another rhyme!" The Queen laughed with delight.

"No, it wasn't!"

"Yes, it was," muttered a noble on the drawbridge who had drunk perhaps too many toasts already. "But not a good one!" he added as the King glared.

"You did! You made a rhyme for me. That's the very first I've had, since you were a—"

"A lad!" the King broke in on her.

"He did it again!" shouted someone in the crowd. There were several tentative cheers from persons unsure if a King who indulged in poetry was something to be encouraged. A man in a strange blue hat shouted "Huzzah!" on the balcony, but disappeared quickly when the King spun to give him a look.

The Queen was beaming now at the King as he forged ahead with his prepared remarks, burying his nose in the parchment and refusing to be distracted again into any accidental lyricism. Gradually the Queen lost her smile as he made no more rhymes and declined even to look at her.

The King finished in a rush and gulped his toast. This was a bad idea, since he was also trying to catch his breath. Everyone was horrified as he began to choke. He tried to assure them he was all right, but this made him gasp and cough all the more. He finally made a "do something!" gesture to the Lord Chamberlain, who bowed low, murmured a respectful "Your Majesty," and smacked him on the back. With a bit of sputtering, he got his breath back.

"It's all right," the Lord Chamberlain called out to the people, "His Majesty just had a frog in his throat."

The Queen burst into tears and rushed into the castle.

❖   ❖   ❖

*They sat in silence* before the great carved fire-place in their private chambers. An embroidery screen stood before her, and she passed the needle from one side to the other, swiftly, efficiently, me-chanically. The fire crackled and popped and occa-sionally settled in more comfortably with a dull *whoomp* and a miniature pyrotechnic display.

She stopped her needlepoint and stared into the fire, remembering. She looked over at the King, who was rubbing his eyes, which ached from studying the treaties, petitions, and correspon-dence that had accumulated like a sand dune against his chair. Her memories were of a time when his eyes had been only for her, when she had filled his life the way his duties now did. He would never have been King of anything but a swamp without her help, yet she was not supposed to talk about what she had done for him.

She longed to tell him how she felt, but what could she say? He could not turn back time. He could not neglect his royal duties. She just wished that, when they were alone, he would have some-thing to say to her. There was a time when he couldn't say enough, and all in rhyme. But now his conversation was only of court matters, which she didn't understand or care about. And so they fell into the great silences.

She sighed.

The King raised his head and regarded her hopefully. "Did you say something, my dear?"

"No," she said, returning to her needlepoint. After a moment, he dropped one urgent matter of state back onto the heap and dug out another.

✦   ✦   ✦

*The King reined in his horse* at the entrance to the royal pavilion. Even at his age, he still liked to dash in at top speed and pull his charger, round eyed and foam flecked, into a high rear just before the tent flap. The vassal duke who was his host on this particular excursion and the rest of the entourage followed at a discreet distance, keeping out of the way while the King indulged his whim.

It was only as he leaned forward to pat the horse's neck and soothe its excited dancing that he realized there was a small, terrified person huddled against the tent wall just beyond the charger's stamping hooves. Strange, in that official visitors would be conducted inside the tent to await him. Anyone else should have been kept away by the guards.

The little man was bowing as deeply as he could while keeping a cautious eye on the still-bobbing steed that loomed over him. His hands wrung a white hat as he moaned, "Forgive me, Sire, forgive me, but . . ."

The King finally recognized the hat as a chef's hat. "What is it, man? If you came for the game, you might have waited a bit." He waved forward an equerry who carried the brace of pheasant that the King had brought down with his arrows. "The deer won't be here for a while."

"Sire, it's not the game, if you'll forgive me . . ."

"I'll forgive almost anything except wasting my time."

"It's about the Queen."

"Come inside." Without a further word, he swung down, tossing the reins to an attendant and leaving the others as he pulled the little man inside with him. The King stopped in an antechamber and faced him, dusting flour from the hand that had gripped the cook's arm. "The Queen. What about her? Quickly!"

"Forgive me, Sire," the doughy little man said again. The King grabbed his shoulders in vexation and shook him, which was a mistake. A dusting of black pepper sifted out of his hair as he was shaken, and he began to sneeze violently. With each explosion, a cloud of white flour rose up around him. His hat fell off and a little dune of salt flowed from it. When he bent to toss some over his shoulder, cinnamon drifted from his collar and sprigs of rosemary and thyme fell from his pockets.

The King stepped back in amazement. "Come, Master All-Spice, you are forgiven. But no more hesitation. A man for all seasonings such as yourself should learn proper measure in all things." This light talk was meant to put the cook at ease, but in fact it froze him in his tracks, trying to decide if laughter at royal jests was compulsory or forbidden.

"Just tell me what you have to say," the King said sighing.

Finally, it came in a blurt. "Your Majesty, I have served my Lord, the Duke, your loyal vassal, for many years now, but I have never before had the pleasure of cooking for your Royal Highness. And so I wished to do some little dish that would give you special pleasure. I have cooked magnificent feasts in my time!" His manner became more confident and oratorical as he launched into this speech that seemed to have been carefully prepared and served often before.

"I have roasted rhinoceros and honeyed the tongues of nightingales with the best of 'em! But it has often been my experience that the simplest dishes can sometimes please a man the best. Even a King, eh?" he added with a wheedling familiarity which the King would have made him regret in different circumstances. "Often something from his youth, some simple, secret pleasure. And so I went to the Queen's tent to ask her if there was something that Your Majesty had especially liked to dine upon in the days when she first knew you."

The King didn't like the sound of this. "And she said . . ."

The little man lost his confidence at that. His eyes widened and his cheeks burned a bright red, as if the spit should be turned so that he would roast evenly. "Well, Your Majesty, first she got a faraway look in her eyes, and then she laughed, and then she cried, and then . . ."

"And then . . ."

"She said . . . or I *thought* she said, it could just be my hearing that has—"

"'She said,'" the King prompted, silently counting to ten to keep from ordering the cook's arrest and execution on grounds of irritation to the Crown.

"'Flies,'" the cook answered finally, shifting from foot to foot in embarrassment and allowing marjoram and curry powder to shower out of his pants legs and puddle around his shoes.

"'Flies,'" repeated the King, dully.

"Exactly what I said!" the cook exclaimed brightly. "'Flies.' And she said, 'Flies' back at me, clear as day. What could I do? I bowed and went away and tried to make sense of it. But I couldn't, and then it struck me that if I didn't serve you tonight whatever she meant by 'flies,' she would be offended, and if I went back and asked again, that would offend her too, so I thought if I could ask Your Majesty . . ." His voice ran down and he broke off in a sweat, which produced a sort of gravy in the floury wrinkles of his neck.

The King thought long before he answered. "You may not know," he finally confided with an unctuous and, to anyone who knew him, extremely artificial smile, "that my wife, the Queen, comes from an ancient Empire, which was where I met her. Their ways of pronunciation are somewhat different from ours. What she was actually saying was 'Fries.'"

"Fries?"

"Yes. Potatoes. In the style of the French *pommes frites*. French fries. Or 'Flench flies,' as she might put it," he added with a laugh that had difficulty escaping his throat.

"Ah!" the cook exclaimed happily as he understood. "Your Majesty likes fried potatoes!"

"Yes, yes, a little secret vice of mine." He ushered the cook to the tent flap. "Very good of you to ask."

The cook drew himself up and announced proudly, "Your Majesty shall have great platters of fries at all his meals until he returns to his own castle." He squinched up his little eyes and leaned in very close. "Or should I say . . . 'pratters of flies'?"

The King laughed heartily and pushed him out.

He rumpled the cook's hair, as if in amusement, but actually to cause him a good, spicy sneezing fit.

The King decided he would have to cut this visit short. He hated fried potatoes.

Almost as much as he had hated flies.

✢ ✢ ✢

*The fire burned* brightly upon the hearth.

He stole a glance at her and saw that she, too, was staring into the fire, hands frozen in midstitch while her eyes gazed at something far away. After several moments, she let out a breath that was a sigh and looked at her hands as if she had never seen them before. Then she picked up the rhythmic movements again exactly where she had left off.

He thought that she was often lost in thought, and often sighed, and had seemed to take no pleasure in work or amusement since . . . he couldn't remember her last smile.

Except when she mentioned the time of their courtship. And that whole topic made him extremely uncomfortable. "What would my people think of me," he had asked many years ago, when they were newly returned to his kingdom, "if they were to learn that their King had an amphibian past?" So they had never spoken of it in public, and the few times she had brought it up in private had just put him in a bad mood. Over the years, it had almost ceased to exist, and that suited him perfectly.

But now, she was beginning to slip and allude to it upon occasion. He wanted to warn her against it, but those moments, so excruciatingly embarrassing to him, were the only times that she smiled, so he just held his tongue and tried to cover over the difficulties that arose.

He wanted to discuss this with her. He wanted to warn her against further reminiscences. He wanted to find out if she was as unhappy as she seemed. And he wanted to say that he loved her.

He looked at her face in the flicker of firelight. So lovely, still, after all these years. Strange, it took conscious thought for him to realize she was beautiful. Her face meant more to him than mere loveliness. It was the face that all his memories wore. When he had ruled wisely, it was her face that had shone. When he had made unforgivable mistakes, it was her face that had absolved him. When he had ridden home in triumph from war, it was her face that radiated the love that gave meaning to death. His own face was a relative stranger to be consulted in the mirror during a visit to the Royal Barber. His likeness in painting and tapestry seemed a work of fiction. It was her face that appeared in every mental image of his past.

He remembered the first time he had seen her face. She came down to the pond near her father's castle and threw a little golden ball, and her auburn hair caught the sun in highlights of gold and red as she knelt and peered into the green depths and he . . .

He refused to think about it.

And he couldn't find the words to say.

And now and then she stared and sighed.

And otherwise, they sat in silence.

✣   ✣   ✣

*The Royal Ambassador* from Rajakhan swept forward as his name was announced and made preparation to bow before the King and the Queen. This was a far more important moment than the casual observer might realize. The Ambassador had been taught from an early age that an Ambassador only *seemed* defenseless, that in fact he was well armed with his weapons which were, in order of importance, Courtly Manner, Wit, and, last and least, Intelligence.

This particular Ambassador had endured long years of practice and rigorous training to achieve and become famous for the quality and magnificence of his bows. Certain insecure monarchs had been intimidated directly into unfavorable treaties without further negotiation, simply by the depth and perfection of his bow. As his mission to this particular King was an important trade agreement for his master, he intended to use his powers to the utmost.

He came to a full halt at precisely the correct distance and pulled up into a rigid immobility. His look was one of fierce speculation, like a particularly humorless wading bird trying to decide whether the thing it confronts in the reeds is potentially dinner or diner. This was the moment in which he gathered all his powers of concentration. Few people realize that a truly spectacular bow is not only difficult, but dangerous in the extreme.

In a sudden blur of motion, he kicked far back with one leg, threw out one arm to the side, and struck himself violently in the stomach with the other, doubling himself in two and plummeting his noble brow toward certain concussion. His body halted its violent descent an inch from the floor, paused in an impossible configuration that could have been slipped under a door, then flung itself straight back up into a rigidity so composed and so similar to the beginning that the naive observer might suppose himself to have hallucinated the entire maneuver. And through it all, even when hovering in full split just above the floor, the Ambassador never lost the air of looking down his nose.

It had been one of his most dazzling performances and he knew it. With fierce, hidden pleasure, he searched the King's face for reaction. The King inclined his head ever so slightly in acknowledgment, maintaining a studiously noncommittal expression. "Mmm," he said.

"'Mmm'?" the Ambassador asked himself. That had been a bow to make an Emperor call for a quill and sign away provinces indiscriminately! The Ambassador stifled an expression of disgust. Had he wasted one of his best efforts on a King so unrefined as not to appreciate it? Yet the King had a fine look about him, a well-robed, handsome man of middle years, who certainly should have learned to appreciate the fine arts of the court.

The Ambassador looked to the Queen, sure that a woman would appreciate his Courtly Manner, particularly one as beautiful even in her middle years as this one. But the Queen stared at a point just above the Ambassador's head and gave no sign of having seen anything at all. He sighed, fearing that this job would be more difficult than he had imagined. Yet all possible situations had been carefully covered in the course of his training. He therefore drew his second weapon, Wit, perhaps not so keen as his first, but still well honed through the grind of long exercise.

"Your Majesties!" he intoned unctuously, snapping his fingers to bring forward two subordinates carrying a mahogany chest inlaid with ivory. "I bring a gift that will, I hope, symbolize the relationship between our two happy countries." The flunkies opened the chest at his gesture to produce a sea-green bolt of beautiful and elaborately patterned silk, which they draped up the steps to the twin thrones. "A relationship as deep as the ocean, as close-woven as silk, and as practical as a length of fine cloth. Properly cut with the scissors of prudence, sewn up with the thread of friendship, and laced with the thongs of mutual advantage, it will make a garment worthy . . ."

The Queen finally glanced at it. Her eyes widened and she burst into tears. The King looked at her in mild distress but remained silent. The Ambassador kept still, wondering if he might have overslept the day this particular situation had been covered.

Finally, the Queen stopped her sobbing to reassure him. "It's nothing. Your beautiful cloth just reminded me of the King, the first time I met him." And she gave the King a very sad and loving look that made *him* stare off into space.

"Wit," the Ambassador reminded himself, trying to regain his grasp of the second weapon. "His Majesty's voice," he suggested, "was as smooth to your ear as is silk to your touch?"

The Queen looked surprised. "Oh, no, His Majesty's voice was quite raucous and unpleasant." She smiled at the recollection.

"Ah," said the Ambassador, feeling increasingly lost in strange waters, yet striving to keep his stroke even. "But his thoughts were as intricate as the web of this weave?"

"Good heavens, no." She laughed. "His Majesty had only one thing on his mind, although he did make it rhyme."

For the first time in his life, the Ambassador had the odd notion that perhaps simplicity was the wisest course. "His Majesty was dressed in silk?"

"No." The Queen tried for a moment to contain herself, then laughed out loud and clapped her hands. "He wasn't dressed at all, but he was all shiny and very, very green."

The Ambassador stood with his mouth agape. Having had Courtly Manner and Wit ripped from his arsenal, he tried to draw his last weapon, Intelligence. And found himself totally defenseless.

So he tried another bow, which was a bad choice given his state of mental distraction.

After a respectful interval, the King decided that the loud cracking noise had not been an intentional part of the bow and that, as the Ambassador showed no signs of regaining a vertical condition, perhaps medical assistance should be summoned.

*The* Queen *was sitting* before the cold hearth when the King found her. He stood at the door, watching her stare into the ashes, and sought for the words to say what he felt.

Why did she long for that time he struggled to forget? Wasn't she proud of what he had since accomplished? He was a great King and he had given her all that she could desire. So why think of those miserable times long gone?

Yet he loved her and wanted her happiness more than anything. He tried to think of what he could do that might give her cheer.

Suddenly, a thought came to him. It made him smile just to think of her reaction. It would say everything to her that he wanted her to hear, that he couldn't say.

He slipped out of the room, quietly, and she never knew he had been there.

✢    ✢    ✢

"*Trust me, my dear,* this is going to cheer you right up."

"But I'm not unhappy," she sighed.

"Yes, I know, precisely, but nonetheless," he responded, a bit unintelligibly, but with great good humor.

He led her through the rose gardens, past the reflecting pools, over the oriental bridge, and into the heart of the yew maze, where she had to take the lead. The Queen had designed these gardens in the early years of their marriage, in those first days of her own blossoming. The King had never been able to find the secret way to the heart of her maze, though he had spent happy hours wandering there. It had been years now since it had been visited by any but the royal landscapers, who kept it in unappreciated perfection.

There was a change. The center of the maze, a bench set in a green and secret place, had been transformed overnight at the King's instructions. Rivers had been bent in their courses at his command, trees had been transported through silence and darkness. Now the last leafy corridor of the maze opened onto the bank of a marshy stream with willows bending overhead and lily pads all abloom in the shallows.

The King gestured proudly. "Do you like it?"

"It's very nice," she replied with a feeble attempt at animation.

"Don't you recognize it?"

"It used to be the yew maze. Now it seems to be a riverbank."

"It's *our* riverbank! This is just like the place where we first met, at the stream that flowed below your father's castle."

She looked around. "There weren't any willow trees there."

He considered them dubiously. "There weren't? Well, I wasn't too sure about that. But don't they look nice? And look, there's your golden ball, just past the catkins by the bank."

"They were rushes and the bank was much muddier. That was why I couldn't get to the ball. And the ball was much larger than that."

"Well, I'm sorry, I seem to have remembered it all wrong, but I did see it from a slightly different perspective. I shall have them change it all tonight and we'll come back tomorrow."

"Thank you for the effort, but it won't really matter. The place was nothing to me."

"But it must mean something to you! You seem to think of what it was like constantly."

"I think of what *you* were like constantly. When I first loved you."

"But look at me now. I've done great things as a King and I may not be the handsomest man in the world, but I'm certainly more attractive than I was in my swamp period."

"Yes, of course, it's just that you're . . . what you are. In those days, you were all the things you *might* be. You were . . . everything possible."

"Haven't I turned out all right?" the King asked, trying to sound light, but feeling more and more desperate to understand what was happening.

"Wonderfully."

"Is there something else you would prefer me to be?"

"Of course not."

"Then what is wrong with me?"

The tears glittered in her eyes, and it was several moments before she could speak. "You are only what you are, and I shall never know your possibilities."

And before he could frame an answer, she fled from him, back through the maze that he had never mastered, while he gazed long and hard into the stream.

✤   ✤   ✤

"Excuse me!" the King called into the darkness of the cave. He could hear little whispers of sound that might have been movement way back in the dark, and a wine goblet lay in the shadows as if thrown aside thoughtlessly. He looked around for some way to announce his presence. He thought of tossing a rock in and calling "Hey in there!" but decided against it. He tried rapping his knuckles on the stone, but it produced almost no sound and was quite painful.

"Knock, knock!" he called, feeling more than a little silly.

After a moment, "Who's there?" was the raspy response.

"The King," he replied, trying to feel more in command than he really did at the moment.

"The King who?" said the voice.

"Beg pardon?"

"The King *who!*"

After some thought, the King decided on a show of importance. "The King who rules over all these lands."

There was a long silence, then a snort. "That's not much of a joke."

"It's not a joke at all."

"Then why'd it start out with 'Knock, knock'?"

"Oh. Sorry. I was just trying to get your attention. I know all the proper ceremonies for entering rooms, applying for admission to strange castles, all that sort of thing. But I'm rather shaky on cave-mouth protocol."

"Oh, ya just chuck in a rock and yell, 'Hey in there!'"

"Really? That doesn't seem very polite."

"Somebody as lives in a cave is probably not a stickler for yer social amenities."

"I suppose that's true. Well, I wonder if I might have a word with you."

"What do ya think ya've been doing the last five minutes?"

"You're right, of course, but . . . Might I come in? Or would you like to come out? I find it awkward speaking to a disembodied voice."

"Oh, well, we wouldn't want anything to be awkward for the King of the Knock-Knock Jokes, now would we?" There were rustlings and stirrings, and a dark, unsettling figure appeared deep in the cave and shuffled toward the light. Whether it was a beast or a man was impossible to determine. It spoke in the voice of an old woman and walked with a curious, three-legged gait as if leaning heavily on a cane. As it approached, the King realized there was no cane, but he couldn't be sure if it had lost a leg or gained one. He began to see details of its face.

"Actually, I don't want to inconvenience you. You might just stop there. If you want."

"Not too awkward talking to me from here?"

"No, no, this is quite acceptable. Thanks very much."

"I'm so glad. Now, what was so important that ya were wanting to have a word about?"

"Well, I don't believe I mentioned it, but this is actually the second time I have been here. I came here once quite a few years ago, quite by chance, when I was out hunting."

"Did ya yell 'Knock, knock' that time?"

"No, I chucked in a rock and yelled 'Hey in there!'"

"Did it get my attention?"

"I should say so. You turned me into a frog. I thought I'd try a different approach today."

The figure nodded its great head. "Good choice. Sometimes I'm a tad irritable."

"Although, perhaps I should have just gone

ahead and done it. You see, this time I *want* to be turned into a frog and I hope you'll help me."

The figure cocked what might be its head at him. "I don't see as why I should," it said, and started to turn away.

"Why not? I only want to be a frog for a bit and it's what you do anyway, so what's the problem?"

The figure snorted. "What I do is turn people into frogs as don't want to be frogs, people what has offended me. I've already done two today, green eyes and a blue hat, picnicking I suppose and tossing their garbage in my cave. Besides, what's the point of turning people into frogs if they *want* to be frogs? Next thing ya know, it'll be all the fashion and everyone'll want to be frogged. I'll just put up a shingle what says 'Froggery on demand' and wait for every two-a-penny duke to come by and chuck rocks at me."

"I don't think everyone would be bothering you to be made a frog. It's really very unpleasant. I know *I* hated it."

The figure looked him up and down. "But ya got over it."

"Yes, and now I'm needing to go back for just a

little while. It's to please my wife, who needs some cheering up."

"Yer wife would rather have ya as a frog?" The King nodded, hesitantly. "Well, why didn't ya send *her* up here to ask me. I'd like to meet a woman with that much sense to her."

"It's meant as a surprise for her. She's been very downhearted these last few . . . well, years, actually. I thought if she could see me again . . . that way . . . it might relieve her nostalgia, help her get over it. Then she could kiss me again and we could get on with it."

"On with what?"

"Why, our lives, of course."

"Sounds to me like that's what she *doesn't* want to get on with. Maybe I should make ya a frog permanently. As a favor to her."

"Oh," the King said, a bit startled. "I'm sure that isn't what she'd want." *I think*, he thought. "Will you do it?"

"Well, yer still missing the main point, which is that I only change those into frogs as irritates me."

"But aren't I being extremely irritating?" the King asked, hopefully.

The figure cocked the great lump on its shoulders and thought a bit. "All right, frog it is. Until she kisses ya."

The King was still worried by the hag's remark about permanent frogdom. "Or until *I* kiss *her*, right?"

"That's not how it works. It's a standard kisser to kissee transference spell: The kiss*ee* acquires the characteristics what the kiss*er* has got. So if ya want to get back to kinging, *she's* got to do the kissing. Still want to chance it?"

The King shifted uncomfortably. "Of course, I have no doubts at all."

"All right, then, yer a frog." And he was. "But if ya come back again, I'm turning ya into a case of heat rash. I don't think there's much chance of *that* becoming fashionable."

✦   ✦   ✦

*Twice upon a time* there was a Frog Prince.

Actually, he was only a Prince the first time, but both times he was very much a frog.

The second time, he was a King, which is what royal tadpoles change into if they manage to evade all the sharp-beaked attendants and serpentine hangers-on that hunt the green pond known as the court. And a mighty King he was, too. A respected King who was good to his people and wise in his dealings and fortunate in his marriage to the most beautiful woman ever seen in the kingdom.

And they all lived happily until after.

✛    ✛    ✛

*The King had been missing* for several days and everyone was wild with concern, including the Queen, who wondered a bit wistfully if he had done something desperate because of her. She ordered the Royal Guard to search throughout the land, but no trace was found. She ordered her serving women to scour the castle, but no secret storing room or turret chamber concealed the King.

Finally, the Queen thought of the little riverbank at the end of the maze and went herself to see if he might be there.

But the bank was empty, and she sat in despair beneath the willows, which bent their heads as if in sympathy with her weeping. What would she do without him? Who would she have to not talk to by the fire? He had been her whole life, even when he ignored her, ever since that day by the riverside, the one that did not look like this one. She had been neglected, but at least she had been neglected *by him*. What would she do without him? And what would become of the kingdom?

Suddenly, a harsh, guttural voice interrupted her thoughts.

*"Why this wailing, why this weeping?*
*Know ye not the one you're seeking*
*Is not dead and is not sleeping?*
*Seek him not in cot or camp."*

The Queen raised her eyes slowly.

*"Fret no more and do not shiver,*
*Look no further than the river,*
*Where you'll find him all a-quiver,*
*Full of love, though somewhat damp."*

She saw in the water a few yards away a little green head with great bulbous eyes. It dived beneath the water, then rose again and spat a little golden ball onto the shore. The Queen clapped her hands together with delight and threw the ball into the deeper water. The frog pushed off with its great back legs and dived down to retrieve it.

Through the whole afternoon the King and Queen conversed and played by the water. His rhyming was a bit rusty, but the Queen forgave him many false rhymes as she felt a rebirth of love such as she had not felt in many years.

"You're so ugly," she breathed, rapturously, every few minutes.

The King tried to take that in the spirit that was intended. It actually wasn't too difficult, since he was having a wonderful time. The Queen was so happy that it made him happy, too. And for the first time in many years, he was not thinking about his kingdom, but only about his Queen.

He did some shameless showing off, leaping mightily into the air, doing all manner of dives, fetching curious stones from the riverbed. He even did a high double backflip to snatch a dragonfly out of midair and then crunched it all up while she made faces of playful disgust. It actually tasted rather pleasant. He thought for a moment of greasy fried potatoes and was nauseated. His memories of his amphibious past had obviously been colored by what he later thought he *should* feel. He was having a wonderful time.

Finally, twilight began to descend and the Queen's smile faded. "I should be getting back to the castle."

The frog hopped, somewhat reluctantly, onto the bank.

"*Night grows thick, enshrouding day,*
*Kiss me quick and let's away!*"

"Oh!" the Queen said. "I hadn't thought of that." And now she looked sad again. "We've had such a lovely day."

A little frown line appeared between the bulging eyes.

"*Had more fun since who knows when,*
*But don't you want your King again?*"

"Of course, my dear," she replied abstractedly, staring off into the maze. She seemed to reach a decision. She turned back and squatted down to him. "Of course I shall kiss you and you shall be my handsome King again and we will return to the castle and life shall continue as it has for all these happy years."

She smiled and looked even more lovingly at him. "But not just yet."

And she turned and skipped up the path into the maze.

✤   ✤   ✤

𝒯*he Queen told everyone* she had remembered

that the King was away for a few days and that she would deal with all matters of state until his return. Everyone was surprised at first, but they soon fell into the routine of presenting their petitions and proclamations at the Queen's levee each morning. She would tell them to return the next day for an answer, and she would spend her afternoons in the farthest part of the gardens, alone. She told her serving ladies that this helped her to think and she must not be disturbed while in the maze. The next morning, she would have a response for each question, and it was usually a very satisfactory one. At first, the courtiers and chamberlains and ministers held back on important matters, assuming that the King would soon return. But after a while they began to bring her everything and, all in all, everyone agreed she did as good a job as her husband had ever done. Although it was strange that her proclamations rhymed.

Which should not be a surprise, since her husband was advising her on everything. At first, he only wanted to discuss when she was going to kiss him. But she would say, "Not just yet," and begin to tell him what was required, and he would forget his own problems in those of the kingdom. If she hadn't needed his help so desperately, it would have made her laugh to see how he would sit on a little tuft of moss and issue decrees.

Until the day she brought him a particularly thorny question of taxation. He pondered it for a while, holding his head this way and that and rolling his eyes about. Then, suddenly, a fresh new mayfly caught his attention and he hip-hop-splashed after it.

The Queen was rather annoyed at this, but then a solution to the taxation problem suddenly leapt into her mind. It was really very simple, once she stopped wondering what the King would do and concentrated instead on what *she* should do. She had never before realized that she might be able to deal with such questions on her own. As she thought about it, she walked off into the maze to pursue her thought and then hurried back to the castle to write it down. For the next several days, she did not get back to the riverbank because she was so busy making her own decrees.

Which did not rhyme.

$\mathcal{S}$*he finally returned* when a point of law was raised that she thought might call for a second opinion.

The King was very sad. He missed having someone to share with, someone to admire and make a fuss over him. He refused to discuss legal issues.

*"You no longer love me,*

  *You're too far above me."*

He moaned, staring up the great height to her face, which seemed stranger than ever to him as he saw it less and less. He remembered her as being lovely, and he held that thought in his mind, yet what he could see of her face was so pale, so flat. Just a little bulge here and there or a tinge of greenness would have improved it ever so much.

"That's not true," she protested. "I'm just terribly busy, that's all. Running the kingdom is a full-time job."

*"I know the worst,*

  *I did it first!"*

The Queen was quite out of patience. She felt some slight twinges of conscience for her neglect of him, but she refused to admit it. "Must you always make poems? I ask for reason and you give me rhyme. They're not even real poems, they're nothing but . . . froggerel!"

He was too hurt even to respond to that. Frogs are very proud of their songs and their voices.

"And stop catching those flies!"

He hadn't noticed flipping his tongue at a passing insect. He guiltily reeled it in and chewed the attached fly as quickly and quietly as he could.

*"I'd thpit it farflung,*

*But it'th thtuck to my tongue."*

It was hard to enunciate with wings sticking out of his mouth.

She departed in a huff. He didn't think to ask for a kiss, and she didn't bother to reply, "Not just yet."

✢     ✢     ✢

Several weeks passed. It was noticed that the Queen had become quicker about making up her mind and her decrees were, if anything, better than the King's. Everyone was satisfied with this state of affairs, except the Queen herself, who now discovered that a little melancholy staring into a fire would be a very pleasant change, but she had no time for it anymore.

She came to realize that she was a good ruler, but there was little satisfaction when there was no one to share it with. She began to understand the role that she had filled for all those years with the King when she thought she had been doing nothing. That, however, did not make her any more inclined to go back to the riverbank in a kissing mood.

Then one bright morning, a new emissary arrived from the Emperor of Rajakhan. He made a point of not bowing, but gave just a most perfunctory sort of nod. He announced that he had been sent to demand an apology for the treatment of the first Ambassador, who had recovered his health but not his profile, which had receded approximately three quarters of an inch toward what passed for his brain since his unfortunate full-frontal encounter with the floor of the throne room.

This literal loss of face had been deemed a great insult by the Emperor, who now awaited a response in the fields just outside the great gate of the kingdom. And, since even Emperors get lonely when they travel, he just happened to have his entire army in attendance, in case any further discussion should be necessary.

The Queen only vaguely remembered the incident. It was her recollection that the Ambassador, in the middle of a perfectly ordinary conversation, had suddenly smashed his face against the floor as if determined to see what was happening in the room below. She felt that the Emperor's demand for an apology was some kind of scheme against the kingdom and called for her loyal vassals to rally with their men-at-arms.

She had often seen her husband (the frog, she remembered with a bit of surprise) riding out to war and looking quite splendid. Mostly, she felt sure, it was a matter of proper wardrobe. She could manage this as well as all the other duties she had taken over.

"This is war!" she thought excitedly. Then she thought with a start, "This is war!" And then a terrible thought occurred to her. "This is war!"

So she informed the loyal vassals when they arrived that she would talk to the Emperor and apologize for whatever slight he had imagined, rather than start a war over nothing. The vassals were outraged. The kingdom's honor was not "nothing." And, incidentally, its army was larger than the Emperor's.

Yet they had a problem. Much as they wanted to go to war, they didn't want to be led by a woman. "Congratulations," the Queen told them. "Now if you will just decide that you don't want to follow a *man* into war either, then the kingdom will begin to have an honor worth fighting for."

The vassals were in no mood for riddles. They conferred and demanded to know where the King was and when he would return.

"What am I to do?" thought the Queen. "If they won't take their orders from a woman, they certainly won't take them from a frog." And so she realized that "not just yet" had finally arrived.

✢   ✢   ✢

"*All right*," *she announced*, arriving at the riverbank, "let's get this over with. Pucker up!" But as she looked about her, she realized the King was nowhere to be seen. She searched up and down, even wading out into the muck of the shallows and turning over the lily pads.

Finally, she sat down on the bank, wet and muddy, and waited. After an hour or so, there was a splashing and the King came into view from upstream, along with two other frogs. He was showing off with her golden ball, flipping it as high as he could with his strong back legs, then shooting it down with his sticky tongue. He stopped when he realized he was being observed, and the other two frogs vanished.

"Ribek," he said.

"Now, don't start on your poetry, because I don't want to . . ." The Queen stopped. "What did you say?"

"Brekik," he replied.

The Queen studied him carefully, the warts, the eyes, all the good-natured ugliness of him. Yes, it was certainly he. "You've been here too long," she said. "It's time to go back. Now get up here and let me kiss you."

The frog regarded her with his steady gaze.

The Queen stamped her foot, forgetting where she was. Her slipper disappeared with a slurping sound into the muck, and her efforts to free it made her lose her balance. She sat down heavily on the muddy incline. For a moment it looked as though she might remain there, held in place mostly by the tightness with which she clenched her brows and the severity of her expression. But then gravity of a different sort took over and she began a slow, stately progression, like a newly christened ship, down the incline of the bank and into the shallows. She finally came to rest with only her head above the ripples.

She tried once to rise, then sat back in defeat. The frog climbed onto a lily pad and solemnly regarded her face from a foot away. It seemed much lovelier to him, now that it was splashed with a nice green layer of pond scum. A tear slipped down her cheek and with a flip he caught it on his tongue. This did not improve her mood.

"What am I to do?" she sobbed. "If I kiss you, you'll come back to the palace and run things again and ignore me again and I'll be left with my needlepoint and my memories. If I don't kiss you, the nobles will probably revolt against me. And even if they don't, it's miserable being all by myself."

The frog regarded her seriously and it's possible that an oily secretion near the corner of his eye was the amphibious equivalent of a tear. Finally, he spoke with an effort, for he had almost forgotten the ins and outs of human speech amid the ups and downs of frog life.

"*All frogs can sing, though no one kisses 'em.*

*We have no kings, and no one misses 'em.*
*We waste no time on war and havoc,*
*But spend it rhyming* kwor! *and* bravik!

*"For all should wait when you've a song.*
*The ship of state will drift along,*
*Whether you be on throne, in bog.*
*So live with me, and be my frog!"*

And he hopped onto her shoulder and before she could draw back *he* kissed *her.*

✢   ✢   ✢

*Ohrice upon a time* there was a Frog Prince. Actually, the last time, it was a Frog Princess. Who was now a Queen. But you get my point. And, of course, in each case, they were actually just frogs, not Princes or Queens or whatever. Amphibians do not recognize royalty.

They were two frogs who had lived in both the court and the swamp and preferred where they were now. Oh, life was not perfect. There were still great cranes and hungry fish and sly serpents to be wary of. But they had all the songs of frogdom to sing, songs like "How Soothing the Mud!" and "With Dragonfly Larvae My Stomach Is Round" and "Where Are You Hiding, My Greenest of Beauties?" Songs that do not translate well into English, but that are quite beautiful in the original language.

And they had the open river and two good froggish friends.

And they truly had each other. That was more than they had had when they were King and Queen of a mighty country. (Which managed quite well without them, I might add. There's always someone willing to be King.)

And they never lacked for a thing to say to each other.

And they lived happily.

A

*Beauty*

*in the*

*Beast*

$\mathcal{D}$*inner was her favorite time.*

She dreaded dinnertime most of all.

Talking to him was always a pleasure, their conversations full of the great paintings she discovered in the far reaches of his castle and the wonderful books she found in his library. And the food, although not as good as her own cooking had been, was plentiful and just needed proper seasoning. The service, on the other hand, was not merely impeccable, it was invisible.

But after dinner would come the inevitable proposal, and that was too much to swallow.

"Beauty," he said, pushing his plate away from him after a passable roast pig in mustard and a delightful discussion of Plutarch's prose style. His voice had the serious tone it held only when he was going to ask the question.

"Beast," she replied, not looking up at him, as she had not all through dinner, unable to bear the sight even while enjoying his words. "He's not even waiting for dessert tonight," she thought, and dreaded his next words because she would have to repay his kindness yet again with discourteous evasion.

She called him "Beast" because he insisted on it. She would never have called anyone such a rude name otherwise. Just as she would never have called someone "Beauty," but that was the name her father had insisted on since she was in her cradle. She had known it as her name long before she knew it had any meaning besides "Hey, you!" Growing up, she was confused to hear people say that she was in the eye of the beholder or that she was only skin-deep. By the time she understood the word's other meaning and grew embarrassed at her name, it had become everyone's habit and too late to change.

Beast said, "I want to tell you a story." The proposal of a story instead of a marriage surprised her so much, she almost looked up from her plate.

"Very well," she replied, pushing her plate to the side. It clattered for a moment over the rough wood of the table and then slid smoothly out of sight. Beauty never tired of seeing this. Or not seeing this, if you prefer. She fancied she could see the outline of the invisible servant's thumb on the rim of the plate just before it was slipped behind an invisible apron. But it happened so quickly, she really just saw the plate one moment and didn't the next.

A glass of wine was caused to appear at her place. The ruby liquid was agitated by the haste with which it had been appeared, and a small splash went over the edge toward her hand. But it never touched her, disappearing as it fell, like rain over a desert. There was an invisible bit of fuss at the rim of the glass and then it sparkled clean again and the crystal rang for a moment as if in song.

Beast waited through all this with a smile, knowing the pleasure she took in it. He had long since lost that simple response to wonders, and he enjoyed watching her. He also hoped that Beauty would meet his gaze, that his new tactic might provoke a new response, but even as she lifted her glass, her eyes stayed deep within the liquid and did not rise to his. He sighed and began his story, which he had thought about all day and was rather proud of.

"There were once two wealthy brothers who lived together because they each cared for only one thing, and that was food. Yet they were as different as they could be, because one was a gourmet and the other a gourmand. The gourmet had the most refined taste imaginable; the gourmand ate everything he could get his hands on. Between them, they kept their chef extremely busy.

"The gourmet often said, 'I live only for the first and last bite: the first bite, for the initial exquisite burst of sensation; the last, for the bittersweet farewell. Everything in between is simply filling.' The gourmand did not often say anything, because it is impolite to speak with your mouth full. But when he did speak, it was usually to curse those same first and last bites because they put limits to his gorging.

"One day each resolved to follow his inclination to its logical conclusion. The gourmet would no longer eat more than two bites of any meal. And the gourmand, who reached this decision in the middle of his post-lunch, pre-tea tide-me-over, would never again cease eating, thereby doing away with both last and first bites at a stroke.

"Their chef was instructed to bring each dish to the gourmet, who would have his two bites and then give all the rest to the gourmand, who then continued with seconds, thirds, and all the ordinal numbers he could cram in before the next meal. For a time, both were extremely happy, but then the gourmet began to feel a bit light in the head, while the gourmand did not feel light anywhere.

"The gourmet became so weak, he actually fainted one day at the sound of a very loud noise. When he awakened, he dragged himself into the dining room to ask for help, but found that the loud noise had in fact been the explosion of his brother, who had finally reached critical mass. There was nothing left of him except one hand, which was still clutching a joint of meat.

"The gourmet rang the bell for the chef, but there was no answer, so he crawled to the kitchen, where he found a note: 'To the Brothers Gourm: I have gone to work for a miserable old miser who will cheat me on my wages and my days off, but when I fix him a meal, he will eat all of it with pleasure and then stop like a normal person.' The gourmet looked around the kitchen for something to eat to give him strength, but could find only the fifths, sixths, and sevenths of what he had already had two bites of for lunch, so he couldn't bear to eat it, but lay down on the hard cobblestones and died.

"Tell me, Beauty, what do you think is the moral of this story?" He felt his point was very clear, and was rather smug that he had wrapped it so neatly in a story.

Beauty had listened at first with some fear, trying to divine the reason for this break from the normal. But the usual pleasure at Beast's voice lulled her, and she was startled when her name broke into the recitation. She thought, "There's no riddle to that story: We must love a thing entire if it is to nourish us," but she did not say that out loud. She ran her fingers along the grain of the wood as if deep in thought.

She finally smiled to herself and suggested, "Opposites detract?"

Beast considered that with a frown. "I suppose the story is not as clear as I had meant it to be." Beast raised a silvered and ornate mirror in his hand and coldly regarded his reflection. Then he turned it toward Beauty. "Will you look at the face I show you?"

She shook her head. "It is too horrible. I can live with it, but I will not look at it. I'm sorry."

"Will you marry me, Beauty?"

Here it was at last. "I cannot answer, Beast."

"Good night, then." Only as he was going through the door did she look up to admire the strength of his dark-robed back and the mane of golden curls.

She knew what the story meant, but it didn't change her mind.

✤   ✤   ✤

"*At the end of his first week* of employment, the chef went to his new master, the miser, and asked for his pay," said Beast, pushing his plate aside into nothingness. Beauty quickly did likewise, although she had not quite finished. Beast was clearly anxious to try again.

"The miser smiled in a very broad and insincere manner and complimented the chef on the food that he had prepared on a very strict budget. He asked to be reminded exactly how much salary had been agreed upon. The chef braced himself for a struggle and replied, 'A hundred shillings per week.' The miser said in a tone of outrage, 'A hundred? Why your work is more worth a thousand than a hundred!'

"The chef was so ready for a fight that he almost rejected a thousand and demanded his hundred as agreed before he realized what he had heard. 'In fact,' the miser continued, 'your cooking is worth more than a thousand. But who can put a price on true artistry? Let us say a thousand and one and leave it at that.'

"The chef was overjoyed at this and nodded enthusiastically, not trusting himself to speak, afraid that he would blurt out one of his most convincing arguments for being paid precisely a hundred and thereby lose his good fortune. The miser wrote the number 1001 on a slate that he always used for figuring instead of paper since the slate could be erased and used over again. Then he looked sharply at the number and squinted up at the chef. 'But what's this? This number is full of nothing!'

"The chef looked at it carefully. He was not good at numbers and reckoning. If a thing was to be measured out in teaspoons and pinches and pennyweights, he was a very terror at it. But these written numbers were a great mystery to him. The miser smiled as he saw the chef studying it out. 'See here, these two round things in the middle, those are zeros, which as you know mean nothing.'

"The chef nodded to show that he was of course very knowledgeable about such things. 'I won't have you being given a lot of nothing in return for all your work, so I'm taking these out.' And he wiped the zeros from the number. Then he unlocked his desk and took out one small scrap of paper, which once had wrapped a bit of meat from the butcher and still had the odd bloodstain here and there, and wrote on it, 'Pay my servant exactly 11 shillings,' and signed it.

"The chef happily took this to the banker in the village and received his money, which seemed much less than he had expected.

"He brooded over this for the next week and was prepared when he went in to see the miser again. The miser again praised his cooking and insisted on paying him even more, *ten* thousand and one shillings this week, and he wrote '10,001' on his slate.

"The chef stopped him before he could go on and took the slate out of his hand. 'You cannot trick me twice,' he said, wiping at the slate. 'Last week you kept the best part and gave me the rest,' he said, 'so this is what you must pay me.' He pointed to the three zeros that remained when he had wiped the two ones away.

"The miser threw up his hands and said, 'Ah, you drive a hard bargain, but you make a tender pot roast, so I must give in.' And he made out his note for exactly 000 shillings.

"Do you see the meaning of this story, Beauty?"

"We must reckon a thing entire if it is to be of value," she thought to herself. Out loud, she said, "Better slate than never."

"Hmm," said Beast, beginning to doubt his storytelling abilities. Then he looked into the mirror and showed it to her. She declined to look and she declined to answer, and he was gone and another dinner was over.

✢     ✢     ✢

"The cook went to work for a mathematician who loved the circle above all shapes. The cook was particularly known for his excellent meat pies, but the mathematician could not bear cutting into them and ruining their perfect shapes, so he could never eat them and wasted away with hunger. Finally, the cook had to bake his pies in square pans so the mathematician could eat away the corners and leave the circles that he loved. So the mathematician cared more for the *appearance* of the thing than for the *substance* of the thing. Now, what do you think this story means, Beauty?"

"It's not much of a story, is it?" Beauty answered, playing with her wine glass. "Not much character development or subplot or . . ."

"Sometimes simplicity is best. Come, now, what does it mean?"

Beauty smiled to herself and blurted out, "You can only determine a mathematician's area if the pies are squared!"

Beast hurled his goblet in fury toward the fire. It disappeared before it was halfway there, spilling out a blood-red arc that vanished before it could sizzle into steam, but on the outermost edge of hearing there might have been little yips of pain from invisibles who had dived into the flames to catch it.

"You are deliberately mistaking my meanings! These stories all show very clearly that you must judge something in its entirety, not by any of its parts, that the outside must be taken along with the inside, that . . ."

"Yes, yes, yes, I have taken your meanings quite well! I *have* heard stories before and can recognize a moral at a hundred yards on a foggy day."

Beast held up the mirror. "Then look here and tell me . . ."

"I will not look at what disgusts me!"

"But as the stories show, appearances are deceptive!"

"So are stories! An artful truth is as deceptive as a lie! Shall I tell you a tale that is full of stories? And every one leads some poor foolish heart on to its breaking through misconception and delusion."

She was talking to the single rose that floated in a glass bowl in the center of the table as if it were Beast she addressed. Anger and sadness battled in her face. He sighed and stretched his hand toward her as if to cup her face, but before he could touch her, the anxious unseens appeared a fresh wine goblet in his cupped fingers.

"Leave us alone!" he snapped curtly, and suddenly they were by themselves, which looked no different from before. "Tell me your story," he said gently.

✣ ✣ ✣

"Tarsen*here was a rich merchant* who lived in the city and had three daughters and three sons. But his business went bad and one day he was forced to retire to a small cottage far away in the forest. Life was different there, quieter and plainer, but all in all it went well.

"Then one day a letter came with the story of one of his ships, which had been thought lost in a storm, returning with a great load of treasure from the East. The merchant gathered his children and told them that he was going to the city and would return with much gold and life would be again what it once was. There was great rejoicing at that. Each of the children made a wish of the present they wanted him to bring back for them. But one of them, let us call her Beauty, could think only of how happy she had been with her father in the cottage every day instead of going off about his business. So she asked for nothing at first but, when teased by her sisters, requested a rose, which was the first thing that came into her head.

"The merchant took what little money they had and made the long, difficult trip to the city. Every night along the way, he would read the letter that told of his great good fortune and then dream of the return of his old life. But when he got to the city, he found that the treasure on the ship had already been seized by the authorities. The letter, which had told the truth but left out all mention of the many suits brought against him since he had left the city, had been sent to get him to return and face his creditors. He had to flee on his old horse to keep from being thrown into prison for his remaining debts.

"On the even longer journey home, he found himself most nights with no food and no lodging under a cruel sky. He would read his truthful, lying letter to stoke the fires of anger in his breast and so survive the cold.

"When he was still several days from home, he was lost in the dark wood in a storm. His horse was near exhaustion and he himself had no food. He didn't know which way to turn, when suddenly a great castle appeared before him. He knocked at the gate. There was no response, but the door opened at his rapping and he entered. All his calls brought no answer, but he found a splendid meal laid out by a fire. He waited an hour, but no one appeared, so he finally ate the meal. Through a little door he found a bed turned down and there he slept. In the morning, there were fresh clothes of his own size laid out and a breakfast before a newly made fire. When he looked for his horse, he found him in a stable, curried and well cared for. In the castle grounds were wonderful gardens, blooming even in the winter. Everywhere he looked was wonder and peace and not a soul to be seen.

"He was, of course, amazed by all of this and thought he had stumbled into a marvelous fairy story, some tale of an anonymous benefactor who did good deeds but kept his identity secret. And so, as he mounted his horse to depart on the last leg of his journey home, he paused in the garden and thought of the presents he had promised his children. He could not bring the clothes of spun gold or filigreed swords, but he found himself in a lane of the most magnificent rosebushes he had ever seen and he thought of Beauty's request. He was sure his invisible host who had given so freely would not begrudge him this, and so he plucked the most perfect of the blooms."

✦   ✦   ✦

$\mathcal{B}$*east made an impatient noise.* "There is a difference between taking something that has been offered freely and simple theft."

Beauty glared at the rose in the bowl. "That may be the point of *your* story, but it is not the point of mine. Do you wish me to continue, or shall we have another of your tales with a moral?"

"Well, there's no need to be unpleasant about it," Beast said, a bit peevishly.

✢      ✢      ✢

"$\mathcal{W}$*hen the merchant arrived at home,* he greeted his children and unlashed from his horse's back a great chest filled with gold and rich clothes and fine swords, which he distributed among them. He gave Beauty her rose and one of her sisters laughed at such a petty thing, but the merchant looked sad and said in a strange voice that the rose had cost more than all the other gifts combined. Beauty asked what he meant, but he shooed her off to assist her sisters in trying on their gowns.

"For three months, the family lived well on the gold and the merchant told them stories of all the wonderful parties he had attended in the city and how carriages would soon be arriving to convey them thence in splendor. These stories were plain lies, but they gave hope and pleasure to his children and so he thought them kinder than the truths he could not bring himself to tell. Only Beauty knew that something was not right, but kept it to herself because her father did not wish to speak of it. She did all she could to make her father happy and always put on the best face she could, poor as that face was. But late at night, when she took out the miraculously still-blooming rose, she also brought out the secret sadness and examined them both together.

"At the end of three months, the merchant called his family together and gave them the truth. They were still poor. They would never return to the city. What remained in the chest was all they had. Some of them sobbed at that, but Beauty was silent, for she knew the true pain was yet to come. Then he told them of the strange castle and of the rose that he had plucked.

"'There was a terrible uproar,' he continued, 'and suddenly the owner of the castle appeared from amongst the rosebushes, and I fell to my knees because his face so overwhelmed me. He accused me of theft and said that these roses were the only things he truly cared for in this world. He said that only a life could pay for the magical bloom. "I meant no harm," I said, unable to look at him. "I am extremely grateful to you, my lord." He said, "Do not call me your lord. I have heard flattery before and I know the falseness of it. Call me 'Beast,' for that is the truth of me.'"

"'Oh, Father,' asked the children, 'what did he look like?'

"'I cannot describe him,' the merchant said, 'but the very thought of his face makes me tremble. I told him the rose was a gift for my daughter whom I loved so well. He asked her name. I said, "I call her Beauty, my lord." That made him pause in his anger, and I told him stories of her sweetness and her good-hearted obedience. Then he told me that I must surely die for my theft, but he would spare my life if I would send my daughter to die in my place. He gave me three months to prepare and a chest of treasure to take with me. And now those three months are gone and I must return to him to die and leave you all on your own.'

"The children wept bitterly, whether for the death of their father or the end of their dreams of wealth it is hard to say. But Beauty shed no tears, simply put on her riding gear and asked the way to the castle. The merchant was horrified, but Beauty would hear of no objection. And the other children prevailed upon him not to leave them orphans.

"So Beauty set out alone for the castle."

✣   ✣   ✣

"*She must have loved him* very much," said Beast quietly.

Beauty shifted uncomfortably. "Oh, she did. But there was another reason. You see, she had been quite taken by her father's story of the castle lord who had everything but was alone, who valued his roses above his gold."

Beast laughed scornfully. "She should have known this Beast cared nothing for roses. They merely suited his purpose."

"Just my point. I am not speaking of what is *true*, I am speaking of what the story made her think. She felt this was a man to whom she could offer something, who would appreciate her as no other had. She had to see this man who called himself Beast, even as *he* wanted to see this woman called Beauty. They were both taken in by stories."

And she raised her eyes to look into his. Ugliness

and physical perfection regarded each other solemnly across the dinner table.

"Why did he call you Beauty?"

"Because he refused to see the truth. He was a businessman who thought he could make something true simply by insisting on it. He forced everyone to call me that, but only he believed it."

Beast's lips parted slightly to reveal the even whiteness of the perfect teeth, which set off the golden tan of his chiseled features. The gentle arch of his brows framed the glint of sky-blue eyes.

He was the very semblance of human perfection. If you judged only by looking.

"We have this in common," he said, "that we are both named for our hearts, not our outward appearances."

She smiled at that, her cruelly twisted lips curling like snakes in the midst of the horror that was her face. If you did not know the pure goodness behind that face, you would have called the smile an evil leer.

He held out the mirror. "You must learn to love this face, as I do. And marry me."

She looked at her reflection. "Oh, I can live with this," she said. "I'm used to it. Although it's still a bit of a jolt when I come upon it unexpecting. But I couldn't live with that." She turned the mirror in his hand so that it showed him his own exquisite features. "Why were you called Beast?"

"I will tell you that story, if you wish, but you will search it in vain for the least hint of a moral."

✢   ✢   ✢

"*I was a very plain man,* an unexceptional man. The only remarkable thing I ever did was to incur accidentally the wrath of a sorcerer who lived nearby. He cursed me in an unknown tongue and told me the curse would be lifted only when a woman married me in spite of what I had become. I slunk away in terror to discover what he had called down upon me. People who saw me in the street stared in what I took to be horror and I was convinced that I had been turned into a monstrosity.

"When I arrived at home, I consulted my mirror with great fear. Judge of my delight when I discovered that I was not a monster but a creature of the greatest imaginable beauty. I was convinced that he had uttered the wrong spell and had blessed me unawares.

"To redouble my pleasure, I discovered that I had but to wish for something and it was mine. Great wealth, rich food, fabulous clothes, all were mine at the merest thought. At first I was in bliss. Before the first night was over, I grew bored.

"The simple acquisition of wealth is inconceivably dull. The miser enjoys his horde because he can put a name and a triumph to every coin. 'These francs were a worn-out horse I traded to a foolish Frenchman. These pounds were a tumbledown palazzo with a fresh coat of paint where a nearsighted Englishman shivered through winter. These drachmas were a Belgian copy of a Turkish carpet foisted upon a cross-eyed Levantine.' Oh, the joy in each of those coins he tells over by candlelight in his darkest cupboard!

"But what pleasure could I have from my wealth? 'Here are the twenty gold pieces I had by wishing at quarter past nine last night. Here the hundred silver from ten thirty and here the thousand copper pennies that were a midnight snack.' I tried out all the largest numbers I knew and then made up even bigger ones. When I wished for a scrumtillion, I had to climb out through the window because there was no space left in the room. I put the money away in cupboards as I acquired it and moved on to the next room, which would appear at my bidding. I never went back to any of those previous rooms.

"Since there was no joy in the money itself, I tried to find pleasure in what I could acquire with it. The greatest artworks and finest furnishings were my prey. Soon I owned everything there was to have in the city where I lived. But what was the pleasure of that? Instead of going down to the main street to see something, I now had to prowl through my multiplying rooms to find where I had left it. And it looked no better or more mine even though it was in my house. Again, I could not say I had created it or had saved from the sweat of my labors to give it value. I merely had to wish for it and it was mine.

"So I tried to find value in people. Surely, with my new beauty and wealth, people must love me and want to be with me. And at first it seemed that way. I gave parties and everyone came and could not get enough of looking at me and listening to my words.

"But I soon found that they looked at me the way they looked at my table, that they devoured me out of greed, not love. My words were tolerated for the beauty of my face and form and there were many schemes to possess both my person and my wealth. Women particularly seemed irresistibly drawn to me, but it was the results of the spell that they wanted, my beauty, my money. Whatever was really me was there simply to be flattered or cajoled or otherwise tricked in the accomplishing of their real purposes.

"I was engaged to marry, several times, each broken off more bitterly than the previous. Despairing, I left my house with all its hidden caches of money for whoever cared to cart them away and wandered off into the world. Wherever I went, people stared at me as at a freak and schemed to own me and my powers.

"I finally found a great forest that suited my purpose and created a castle in its midst. I longed for solitude, but even here I was pursued. Women sought me out, men of business came offering deals. Even those who arrived by accident quickly tried to acquire me or some bit of me.

"So I acquired them instead. I had always been a good sort of person, in an unthinking way. How bad can you be when you have no money and no power? You drift along being generally virtuous because your well-being depends on the goodwill of others and you hug your small vices to your secret self. But now I had wealth, power, and monstrous beauty. I was sought after instead of seeking. So I set tests for my visitors and they all failed. And when they failed, they became mine."

✢ ✢ ✢

*Beauty stared at him,* uncomprehending. He looked back and an evil grin gradually grew on his face.

Suddenly he hurled his wine glass over one shoulder. It vanished halfway to the wall, and the scarlet smear of wine was wiped away as it cascaded toward the wood.

But one drop struck and stained the grain crimson like the evidence of murder.

Beast gestured toward the emptiness. There was only silence, yet Beauty's skin crawled as she didn't hear but *felt* a scream of pain filling the nothingness in response to Beast's casual gesture. For a moment she thought she saw a small man in a curious blue hat before he disappeared into his invisible world.

She turned to Beast, eyes newly filled with horror as he grinned at her. "Who are these invisibles that serve you?"

"They are my race of wooers, my would-be wives and business partners, changed by my magic into perfect servants, silent, unseen, unable to deny my slightest whim. They were as real as you or I when they came with their lies of how they wished only my happiness. Some I almost believed, to my pain. But eventually the truth would appear, and then," he laughed, "they wouldn't. I very kindly let them fulfill their professed wishes by staying to feed my happiness in ways they could never have imagined.

"Your father was not the first to pick a rose in my garden, to take the one thing that was not offered. Many have come with love on their tongues but greed in their eyes, and stayed to clean up my messes. Even as the story spread of those who entered my house never to be seen again, they continued to come, each convinced that he or she was the one clever enough to win the prize, to control the unlimited power and wealth.

"And to my face they called me 'Sir' and 'My Lord' and 'Dearest love.' But behind my back they called me 'Beast.'

"And I became the thing they thought me.

"Now tell me, Beauty, where is the moral of that story?"

She spoke quietly. "The moral is where it belongs, at the end, to which you have not yet come. What that moral will be lies in your hands to determine."

Beast shook his head. "My end is written on my face, as is yours. Cold and heartless and inhuman I shall remain because no one will really see me, only what I look like. No one will love me for what I am, only for what I can do. If they give to me, it is only to take. So I shall return their investment of cruelty with interest."

"You have never been cruel to me."

"You have never sought to use me. Not yet," he added, his face twisting suddenly so that for a moment Beauty seemed to be looking in a mirror.

He calmed himself with an effort. "And what better than me can you hope for with . . . your face? Don't you see that the last, best hope for both of us is each other? We both know the vanity of external appearances. Beauty and ugliness are the same thing, a chance shaping of the physiognomy that causes the great mass of humanity falling between the extremes to turn and gape like the monkeys they are. Will you marry me, Beauty?"

She looked at him carefully. "Why do you wish me to marry you?"

"Because you are my last chance. All the others wanted me *because* of what I had become, not in spite of it. You are the only one I have found who can break the spell and make me an ordinary man again. Perhaps, with your help, I can heal my soul."

She looked at him with terror. His words spoke of hope, yet his voice was full of despair, and his eyes brimmed with anger and hatred, as if he longed to destroy the thing that could save him.

"I do not think it is in my power to heal you. Good night, Beast." And so saying, she hurried to her room.

✢   ✢   ✢

$\mathcal{S}$*he tried to sleep that night,* but in the darkness she kept remembering those eyes brimming with hatred and pain and love and anger. Horror filled her, and she knew she could not bear to look at him again.

As she tossed and turned in her canopied bed, she suddenly noticed the silken sheets twisted around her. She pulled a length between her fists and snapped it tight. It was strong; it could make a rope strong enough to hold her weight.

At first, she had great difficulty with the twisting and knotting of the slippery material, but then invisible hands came to her aid.

"They are happy to help me against him," she thought, wondering who was helping her, a woman who had wooed him for his wealth or a businessman who had schemed to defraud him. Or just a poor blooming idiot who had picked a rose.

She had been so happy with the invisibles before. It had been a comfort to be surrounded by persons whose faces did not gaze at hers in hideous fascination or turn away in disgust. She had always felt that they were sympathetic to her in some way.

But now that she knew their history, she felt their faces held the same disgust as all the others, they were just hidden from her. She started to send them away so that no one should look upon her.

But then she thought there was one thing worse

than showing a face of great ugliness to the world and that was showing no face at all. And she spoke kindly to them and worked with their help to effect her escape.

She climbed one of the great oak trees, from which she could reach the wall encircling the castle. With the help of unseen fingers, she tied the rope securely and prepared to lower herself over and down the wall.

A light appeared on a lofty battlement of the castle. A tall, straight figure held a torch high. He raised his hand toward her and she thought of those poor, disappeared would-be brides and business partners. She hurled herself over the edge, slid down quickly, dropped to the ground, and ran away through the trees.

A terrible voice wailed behind her. "Beauty!" it cried, and dropped to a tearful whisper, so perhaps she did not hear the rest of what it said aright, but it sounded like "I would have opened the gate for you."

✢　　✢　　✢

*Her family greeted her* with surprise and delight. Perhaps there was rather more surprise than delight for most of them, but her father's happiness made up for the rest.

A great feast was spread for her in celebration. Actually, it was a poor meal in comparison to those she was used to in the castle of the Beast, but it was all the little cottage and its gardens could provide. And if marrow root was the only plentiful component and not a sauce was to be seen, yet it was seasoned with joy and familiarity and Beauty was well pleased.

Her father tucked her up that night in her own little bed in her own little room below the stairs. She was touched that he had kept it just as she left it. In truth, no one else had wanted the cramped, airless little space for their own, and it had been safe at least until the potato crop was brought in.

She lay alone for a while with one little candle flame flickering. "This is where I belong," she thought. "This is where I am loved. Or at least accepted as I am."

But her heart gave a leap when she noticed on the little chest the glass in which there still bloomed the rose that had been the cause of so much. Only a life could pay, Beast had said. But surely he would not follow her here once he had let her go. If he wished to harm her, he would have done it then. She shivered at the thought of joining his invisible staff of servants. To have no face, no identity, seemed more horrible to her than her own fate. But she felt reasonably sure that it was over with, and she thrust all her misgivings away and blew out the candle.

Yet even in the darkness, her eyes stole ever and again to the same spot where the rose should be. The more she stared, the more she fancied there was a slight glow about it. She began to think she could not sleep with that costly flower floating eerily before her sight. But, strange to say, before the thought was fully formed, the soft radiance had soothed her deep into a sweet-dreaming slumber.

✤　✤　✤

*Life quickly settled back* into routine, which made Beauty glad. Since her sisters and brothers cared nothing for housework, the little cottage had fallen into something of a shambles. So Beauty threw herself into it with a will, cleaning, dusting, polishing. Her brothers and sisters would pretend to be annoyed by all her bother, but they were quick to point out any little places she had missed.

She went to bed tired, but it was a happy ache that pulsed through her as the rose glowed in the dark. She was home.

Then one night, when she had been back a week, she finished her dinner first as usual and got up to clear. She was listening to the conversation, which was as always about the business deals her father had pursued. If even one of them had just turned out as expected, all agreed, the family fortune would have been made. That led to the villa they would have had on the seacoast and the dresses the sisters would have worn to the finest balls and the positions of military honor and prestige the brothers would have purchased.

Beauty was idly remembering her talks with Beast, conversations full of art and literature. She felt a little wistful but told herself that she had lost some things only to gain much in their stead, a home and a place where she knew who she was and everyone else knew her as well.

Just as she leaned in to pick up her brother's plate, he pushed it to the side without pausing in his description of imagined feats of purchasing power. Without slowing its movement, she scooped it smoothly to the top of the stack she carried and felt some little pride at the neatness and efficiency of her actions.

Suddenly, it struck her where she had seen such efficiency before and she stopped dead for a moment. One of her sisters drained the last drops from her mug of water and raised it behind her. Before she realized, Beauty was there pouring from the water pitcher and balancing the plates on her other arm. Her sister brought the mug back to her lips and drank again without ever once looking around.

"Father!" she cried out in horror. Conversation ceased and all turned questioning eyes to her.

"What is it, Beauty?" her father asked.

"Can you see me, Father? Have I disappeared?"

The others made little noises of irritation, and her father cleared his throat before he answered, "Of course, Beauty. I mean, of course I can see you."

"Then why don't you look at me?" she asked.

"But I am looking at you," he said, confused, with his eyes focused just above her right shoulder. As she realized now they always were, always had been. Even when he called her Beauty, he never quite looked at her. None of them ever really looked at her. She had thought she was coming to the place where her face did not matter, where she was accepted for herself in spite of her appearance, but she realized in that moment that she was accepted only as a movement in the corner of one's eye, an action completing itself and departing before one's attention was allowed to turn fully toward it.

She was invisible to them.

Beauty tried to think of what to say to cover her horror and confusion, but she needn't have bothered. After a few irritated glances had been exchanged, the conversation resumed and her interruption might never have happened. She slipped among them, clearing, wiping, cleaning, and they never saw her. A little later Father sent one of the sisters to help Beauty with the dishes, but they were already done and Beauty had disappeared into her room.

She huddled over her little candlestick for a long time, trying to see what she should do. Beast had done cruel things and his face tormented her with its beauty, but he spoke to her as a person and he looked at her, even if he saw her face as a symbol instead of a face. She loved her family, but she was

no more than one of Beast's invisible servants to
them. Even, she sighed, to her father, who upon
occasion made a great show of his love. She realized now it was the same way he praised some of
his bad business deals that he insisted were good,
sound investments that had merely met with a little hard luck.

Where could she go? What could she do? she
asked herself again and again and received no response. The little candle finally guttered and went
out, and she sat in the darkness, dreading and yet
anxious for the faint glow of the rose to appear.
Perhaps its gentler light could show her an answer.

But many minutes passed and she saw no glow.
She squeezed her eyes shut to force them to become accustomed to the darkness. She saw the
darting lights and comets that scuttle behind the
eyelids, but no roseglow.

She fumbled through the darkness to pick up the
glass and hold it before her eyes. Even with her
nose touching the rim of the glass, there was nothing to see. Where was the glow?

She threw her door open. All had gone to bed,
and there was darkness everywhere. She felt her
way to the kitchen and tried to see the rose by the

faint embers left on the hearth, but she could not. She grabbed up a twig from the woodpile and thrust it into the coals and blew so hard her ears popped and crackled. At last the twig caught fire, and she held it beside the glass and could see.

Dry and shriveled it floated in the water. As she gazed, a petal curled and fell away from the bloom. It joined others forming a lifeless carpet on the water. Only a small clump huddled together in the heart of the rose, tight–clamped like a fist slowly releasing hold of something.

Only a life could pay for the magical bloom. That was what Beast had told her father. Now the price was being paid, but not with Father's life, nor with hers.

"Beast is dying," she said into the darkness.

✢ ✢ ✢

*There was a man she loved* who loved her back, she told her father in his half-waking stupor. Her father assumed it was some servant at Beast's castle, probably some poor crippled or malformed creature who welcomed her assistance, and she did not correct his notions.

He hugged her to him in the darkness. With his

face pressed next to hers, he stared over her shoulder and told her he loved her. Beauty thought sadly that that was all he had ever seen of her anyway.

Then she was on their poor horse and riding.

The way was long and hard, but she did not rest. She drove the horse to exhaustion and beyond, using it cruelly, feeling its every pain in her own body. When it could go no further, she ran on with no more thought for her bleeding feet than she had had for its faltering hooves.

In her hand she held what remained of the rose, clutched as if she could hold springtime in the bloom by the tightness of her grip. Yet ever and again, when her hand cramped and her fingers parted in spasm, another petal would slip away and fall to be ground into the mud by her stumbling feet.

She staggered on in a daze, uncertain now where she was or where she was going. She was sure only that she would know it when she arrived.

Finally she raised her eyes and saw the gate to Beast's castle. But those mighty, impassable doors were shattered and hung awry on their hinges. As she watched, one crashed to the ground, carrying a ragged patch of wall with it.

Fearfully, she passed into the garden and beheld a scene of chaos, as if wilderness had reigned there for a hundred years instead of a week. Great thorns choked flowers and trees, and roots shattered the ornamental walkways into fragments of stone and brickwork. Pools and fountains had cracked their rims and run together in a swampy morass. The stone frogs that had spouted water from happy mouths were now drowned in the muck by those gapes they could not close.

She plunged into it all and fought her way through by ways she did not know. She was conscious of neither peril nor pain, knowing only the need that pushed her ever forward.

She found herself standing at the door to the castle. She looked around in wonder. The thorns grew high on the walls and there were great holes everywhere. One entire wing had collapsed in upon itself, and even as she listened she could hear the crash of masonry at a distance.

She looked down at the ruin of her clothing, at the green of swamp scum that covered her. It mingled with redness flowing from terrible ragged wounds that she just now began to feel.

The strength was slipping from her and she

knew suddenly that she was dying. She was surprised to see her clenched fist. It did not seem a part of her. She admired its strength, the last that lived in her body. And even as she watched, she felt it departing. Her hand opened slowly, and a small drift of petals swept away on the fetid wind.

"Beast!" she cried. And her body collapsed and rushed down toward the oblivion that it craved. But some last, deep part of her being pitched her forward so that her small, crumpling weight struck the great door of the castle.

It was enough. The door groaned the anguish of unaccustomed weakness and fell inward. There was no crash as it broke apart into dust even as it fell.

On a plain chair in the hall sat Beast. His head drooped to the side toward the wing of his castle that had already collapsed. With a great effort, he raised that paradigm of beauty and gazed through perfect, clouding eyes at the little figure on his doorstep.

He pulled himself up straighter. As he did so, more crashes resounded from other chambers, and the sounds were closer than before.

He extended his arm, shaking with the effort.

His gesture was almost the same as that which had struck down an invisible being with unspeakable anguish in another time. There is very little difference amongst magics.

He concentrated what remained of his will and energy and brought all his being into that gesture. He held it for a moment and the terrible grindings and rumblings came rushing forward.

His hand sank down and he slumped back into his chair. And what remained of the castle came crushing down.

Dust and debris filled the air for many minutes. When they began to settle, there was only a great twisted mass of stone and timbers to be seen. All the glorious working of rock and woodgrain were brought to splinters and gravel.

But in the midst of the wreck, there remained two clear spaces that the once-enchanted stones had maintained in deference to their former master, who had perhaps ruled stone more kindly than flesh.

After a time, Beauty stood up in her circle of stone and looked down at herself with wonder. Her wounds had been healed by that last magic of Beast's, and she seemed to have passed through a dream, a dream of a dark tunnel to a light and a great longing to go there.

Then she saw Beast seated in his chair, circled by his court of stone, and she shook off the last of the dream to rush to him. She knelt beside him and crossed her arms on his knees to look up into his face. She looked desperately for some sign of life.

With a trembling voice, she pleaded, "Ask me to marry you, Beast."

There was no response. His perfect eyes remained closed and the expression on his perfect face was of an exhaustion beyond the power of sleep to heal.

"Are you going to give up so easily?" she shouted at him. "You always wanted the answer to that question. Are you going to let mere death cheat you of it?"

The glorious head rose slightly, and there was just a glint between the long lashes. The perfect arches of the lips moved slightly and a breath whispered past the even whiteness of the teeth.

"Will you marry me, Beauty?" she heard, faint as the whisper of leaves in the forest of dawn.

She caught a shuddering breath and tried to still

the beating of her heart.

"Maybe," she answered, very definitely.

His head sank and there was no movement in his chest. Beauty watched anxiously for some moments. Then, "Beast?" she asked.

He raised his head and looked at her with a surprised expression. "I feel better," he said.

✢   ✢   ✢

*He quickly recovered* his strength in her presence, and he used his renewed magic to create a little room for them in the midst of the ruins. She refused to answer any of his questions, but said to him instead, "Let me tell you a story.

"There was once a cook . . ." she started.

"I fear," said Beast, "that the apothecary is going to be dosed with his own potion."

"Who had held three positions," she continued undaunted, "and none had worked out to anyone's satisfaction." This with a little shake of her head at Beast, who nodded like a schoolboy accepting his punishment.

"One day he took a post with a scholar of great learning. On his first day of service, he made a perfect little cake. It was iced in beautiful swirls of chocolate fudge and had jam between the moist and fluffy layers of lemon angel food, and just when you thought you had tasted it all, you came to the fresh strawberries hidden at its heart. He was very pleased with his creation as he brought it to his new employer in his library. The scholar gestured him to put it down without looking up from his manuscripts. The cook did so and backed away.

"But, as he was anxious to know if the scholar was pleased, he hesitated in the doorway to watch. The scholar continued in his studies for a good while and muttered to himself as if he had a problem that wasn't admitting of easy solution. He pored over manuscripts and books and still grumbled and knit his brows. The cook began to fear that nothing would please him in this mood.

"Then the scholar turned away to another shelf and a volume of heavy lore fell from a high perch and landed precisely on the cake. Hearing the noise, the scholar turned back and was amazed to find the book he wanted lying right there before him in the ruin of the cake. He grabbed it up happily and flipped through the pages.

"The cook was horrified. He was trying to make

a good impression and here was this smashed bit of pastry, more pancake now than cake, oozing strawberries and jam from the wounds in its crumbled fudge icing. But the scholar took up the cake on its plate and ate with delight as he read the words he had been seeking. He laughed and ate every crumb, and when he closed the volume with a satisfied smile, he even licked the fudge off the back cover. When he noticed the cook in the doorway, he gave a little wave and said, 'Excellent cake! Give me more like that and we shall get on well.'

"Now, Beast, where is the moral of this tale?"

Beast thought, "The appearance doesn't matter as long as we find what we seek within." But he said out loud with a grin, "Always fudge a book by its cover."

Beauty smiled. "Look at this face I show you. Tell me what you think of it."

"It is the mirror image of the world's . . ." Beast began quickly, when Beauty stopped him.

"Look at it when you speak of it, not past my shoulder."

Beast looked at her squarely. "It is the symbol . . ." he began.

"Tell me no symbols, tell me what you think of it."

Beast drew a deep breath, then gave her a nervous smile. "It's very ugly," he said.

Beauty smiled. "Good. Now we can begin to be true friends. Tell me, where are your servants?"

"They are gone. I gave them back their physical forms and all the gold they could carry, and transported them to wherever they wished."

"Why did you do this?"

Beast sighed. "I had always felt justified in punishing them, that my cruelty simply mirrored their own. But when I told you my story, when I saw the pity you felt for them, I felt . . . ashamed."

She smiled. "Then you have already begun to heal yourself. You don't need me at all."

"I don't need you for what you can do for me. I need you for what you are."

Beauty was pleased. "Good. Then I'll stay, but not as your wife, just as your friend. With the invisibles gone, the housekeeping will give me something to do and the meat will finally be seasoned properly. You should consider taking up a hobby yourself.

"As to living arrangements, you shall create a little cottage here with a room under the stairs for me. That's what I'm used to. You may do what you like with the upstairs, where you will live. Make it a palace if you like. We shall continue to meet and converse every night at dinnertime and you shall ask me occasionally to marry you and I shall probably avoid direct answers, but you must never give up hope."

"But Beauty," Beast protested, although he was pleased with what she proposed, "if you never marry me, the curse will never be broken. I shall never again be what I once was."

Beauty looked very serious. "You mean you will never again be a plain, commonplace man? You will always retain your magic powers and physical perfection?"

She smiled broadly. "We'll just have to put up with it, won't we?"

A

*F*ate

*in the*

*D*oor

"*You're selling something, aren't you?*"

"No, you have my word. It's an important survey, just a few questions for our statistical records."

"Yes, well, we're not interested, I'm afraid, whatever it is."

"We? You have a husband? Is he at home? Perhaps I could speak to him . . . ?"

"He's not available just now. So, if you'll excuse me . . ."

"Please let me in! It's really, really important." He pushed his way past her to stand in the tiny hallway. She watched him warily, ready to shove him out if he said the wrong thing. He watched her very closely in return. He clearly had experience at being thrown out of cottages.

"It's just, you see, I've been all around this part of the country and no one wants to answer my questions, it's only a few simple questions, I have to ask them, if I don't get answers, I just, you know . . ." His voice ran down into a mumble and his head sank, but his eyes peeked up at her and they were bright and watchful even as his voice tried to be pitiful.

She gave a shrug and a sigh. "Oh, who cares, ask your questions." She led him into a tidy little sitting room that was remarkably free of any clutter. She sat on a chair while he paced nervously.

"I hope these few questions are easier to answer than they are to ask," she remarked, feeling more cheerful as his mood grew worse.

Finally, he turned directly to her and blurted, "How old are you?"

"Why do you want to know?"

"Statistical verification," he answered with a smug little smile, as if that magic phrase opened all doors. When she did not immediately reply, he began to whistle tunelessly, as if the answer were really none of his concern.

"Most people," she finally said, slowly and carefully, "would say I was about forty-six."

"And your family background: would you say that you had been raised as a member of the serf class, lesser nobility . . ." His voice was rising in excitement. ". . . a major vassal lordship, or royalty itself!" His hands flew out in an expansive, encompassing gesture.

She looked at him hard, deflating his excitement. "Demographically speaking," he finished, with a final weak flutter of one hand.

"You don't write my answers down?"

"I can remember them."

"I think you should go," she said.

"Your husband . . ." he responded quickly.

"Not available," she snapped back.

"But if he were available, how old would he be?"

Her eyes clouded over and she looked away from him.

"So," he said with mounting excitement, "he's not 'not available,' right? That is, he *is* not available, but not in the sense of 'apt to be available again at any moment.' In fact, his lack of availability is a permanent condition, right?"

"If he were available," she said softly, "his age range would be in the forty-five-to-fifty category."

"But since he stopped being available, doesn't

he fit better in the ageless category, or perhaps I should say the all-ages category, right? I mean, to put it precisely, he's dead, isn't he?"

She looked at him long and hard. "Yes," she replied coldly, "in a statistical sense you could call him dead."

The man laughed. "Perfect! I mean, for the statistical profile." He tried, too late, for a sympathetic tone. "I mean, I'm very sorry personally, but you know statistics. Those little numbers just keep tumbling along no matter how we feel about them." He laughed with a rising note of hysteria.

She snorted. "You should be tumbling along yourself before your own statistical profile catches up with you. You're not exactly a young man. Accidents happen."

"Well, yes, but mostly in the home."

"This is my home. What better place for something to happen to you?"

He swallowed nervously. "One more question, just one. Your first name, just for our records." He smiled weakly.

"Aurora," she said with a little sigh.

"Fine," he said. "That's just fine. Not so hard, was it?" He stood straighter suddenly and seemed more resolute in his actions. "I'll just clear out of here now and let you get on with your business. Woman's work, eh? Never done," he said, chuckling.

He headed back into the hall and put his hand on the door latch, where he stopped. "Oh, just one more little thing."

"What is it?" she asked, stopping and bracing herself to shove him out if need be.

"I have to kiss you!" he blurted, and reached for her with arms and mouth outstretched. But her reflexes were good and the heavy walking stick by the door was close to hand, and he was limping around in the front yard before his lips had lost their pucker.

He hobbled back toward her, but she slammed the door as he leaned into his forward rush. There was a good solid thump right at face level, which made her smile as she threw the bolt.

"You don't understand," gasped the slightly bruised voice behind the door. "I have to kiss you! I know who you are."

"I'm a widow living quietly in a small village. That's all I am now. If you have to kiss that entire demographic cross-section for your survey, you're going to wind up with a major case of chapped lips."

"You don't understand!" he repeated. "I've been waiting twenty-five years to kiss you! You're not forty-six, right? You're really a hundred and forty-six, correct?" Her gasp made him rush on with growing confidence. "You were cursed by an evil fairy, am I right? You slept a hundred years, waiting for a prince to come and wake you with a kiss, right again? Am I on a roll or what! Well, here I am. I'm a prince, I've got identification, and I've come to kiss you!" There were several seconds of silence before he finished less surely. "So, open the door. What do you say, huh?"

Her mouth was screwed up tight and her eyes almost burned a hole through the door when she finally spoke. "You're twenty-five years and one good husband too late! I've already been awakened . . . maybe with a kiss, who knows. Anyway, I woke up, and there he was. We had a good time, talked to a dragon, hung out in a cave, did a lot of nice things. Then he died and it took a while, but I got used to it, and now I've made a life for myself here. So I certainly don't need whatever you're selling."

"But I need you," the voice said plaintively. "I heard he died. I tried to be sorry, but I couldn't. I knew it was my last chance."

"Chance for what?" she asked, and when there was silence, she repeated it. "Chance for what!"

His voice, when it came, reached out to her more softly, and it had a ring of truth it had not worn before. "Twenty-five years ago, I was on my way to your castle. Wake the Sleeping Beauty, that was all I could think of, all I'd thought of since I was a tiny princeling. I prepared for years. I practiced all kinds of weaponry, mastered the complicated double roll/thrust for dealing with dragons, studied botany and garden maintenance with an emphasis on thorn elimination, took trumpet lessons to strengthen my lip technique . . . I was ready for everything. Except . . ."

"Except?" she asked suspiciously, unwilling to admit he had caught her interest.

There was a little growl from the other side of the door. "There was this girl," he muttered in an undertone.

"Aha!"

"It's not what you think! At least I think it's not what you think. I think. She was a nice girl."

"And she made you break training. Did she offer to help with extramural lip exercises?"

"No, nothing like that. I met her in the woods when I was on my way to find you."

"Even better. Don't tell me, I think I know this story. She was lolling about in some sun-dappled meadow, am I right? Claimed to have lost her sheep? Didn't know where to find them?"

"No. Actually, she was in a glass coffin."

That stopped her for a moment. "Well, she gets points for originality, at least."

"She'd eaten a poisoned apple, and there she was all stretched out, looking so pale and beautiful, I thought I should try to help out. And, besides, it was a chance to practice my kissing. I'd worked pretty much on a theoretical level up until then. How was I supposed to know she'd wake up and all the birds and animals and everything would come pouring out, congratulating us and making plans for the wedding? A bunch of irritating bluebirds threw together a wedding dress before I could even introduce myself."

"You could have run away."

"Easy for you to say. You didn't see the guys she was keeping house for. They were small, but there were seven of them and they looked mean, with all kinds of pickaxes and stuff. I finally decided, 'Well, what the heck, you wake up one, you wake up another, what's the difference, you know?'"

"Thank you so much."

"But the years went by and I just kept thinking I had missed my big chance, the one really meant for me. I mean, I was happy enough. Except maybe for living out in the woods. And the seven guys always . . . No, I was happy. I admit it. But I kept thinking, 'This isn't what you were meant for. You were supposed to go on to that castle and kiss that other one and live in the palace and have a very different life.'"

"We never lived in a palace." She sat on the floor with her back against the door. She was smiling. She seldom dwelled on the past, but she found it oddly pleasant to think back on those days with this stranger, as long as the door was between them.

"We consorted with a dragon and lived in caves and had more gold than you could dream of, but we never bought anything with it." She heard him settling down on the porch to listen, could tell from the sounds that he was leaning his back against her own with only the width of the door between them. "We forged it into glittering hooks that required no bait to lure the royalty among fish. And we spun it into clothes that shone like the sun but dented at the touch of a fingernail. And we stretched it out into whisks to brush cobwebs from the corners of the cave."

She was about to tell him of their years after the dragon, but she heard scuffling sounds through the door. She was irritated. "What are you doing?" she called, getting to her feet, her mood broken.

"Excuse me," he said, panting somewhat. "Do you own a pig?"

"Yes," she replied, with some pride. "A big, spotted hog named Iggy. If he's roaming around in the yard, just ignore him. He's broken out of every sty I've ever built for him, but he never runs off, just enjoys freedom in a technical sense. Don't worry about him."

"Well, normally I wouldn't," was the winded response, "but he has already eaten the laces out of my right boot and seems determined on the left for dessert."

She threw the door open and looked down at the stranger rolling around in the mud with Iggy, who clearly enjoyed the company. She laughed, then put on a strict face and scolded the pig back to its pen in the side yard, replacing the wooden latch. Iggy stood against a far wall, grunting gently in wide-eyed ignorance of how the gate had ever gotten open and chewing meditatively on the remnants of two bootlaces.

She returned to the front yard, where the stranger was pouring mud out of his boots and slipping them back on. "Iggy likes you," she announced, "and he's a good judge of people. We'd better find you something other than mud to hold your boots on with. Come on into the house." He rose quickly and followed her, then went back to stick his feet into the boots, which had elected to stay behind. He followed her, walking on the sides of his feet with his toes scrunched.

She stopped suddenly and looked back at him. "But don't even think about kissing." He held up his hands in a mute protestation of innocence.

She led him again to the remarkably neat little sitting room, where this time he sat while she went to a door opening off it. She glanced back at him with something like nervousness, then carefully braced her shoulder against the door before turning the latch. The door thrust suddenly against her, as if some long-imprisoned creature had just sensed its chance for freedom. But she held it there and allowed the door to open only wide enough for her to slip her hand in and grope about.

"I think . . . there's some string . . . you could use . . ." She panted with the effort of reaching and holding at the same time. "Just a little farther . . ."

But that was a little too far. The door gave a triumphant rusty screech and flung itself open. She leaped back just in time to avoid the waterfall of household debris that poured into the room. Old pots, perfectly good except for missing a handle; odd bits of wood sure to be useful someday; lengths of cloth and yarn, too short to use, too long to throw away; shattered broom handles tumbling after the broom heads, which still clutched their stumps and waited for guidance. All cascaded into the room to drown two chairs and an end table and wash up around the unlaced boots of the survey taker.

They were silent through several aftershocks as clumps of half-balanced flotsam gave up and took the plunge to join their brethren on the floor. Then she turned where she stood, ankle deep in years of homely accumulation, and grinned sheepishly at him. "I never did get the hang of housekeeping."

He nodded sympathetically.

"To tidy a room up," she explained, "you always had to put things someplace else, which just made that other place messy. And if you tidied *that* up, then half of it went back to the first place, so what was the point? Everything always belonged someplace else, so I finally just declared this closet 'someplace else' and put it all here. Which works very well," she added defensively, "as long as you don't actually have to take anything out. It was better when my husband was alive. He had a natural gift for housecleaning. I mean, you wouldn't think a cave could ever bring the word 'spotless' to mind, now would you? What were we looking for?"

He couldn't remember either for a moment and crossed his legs as he thought. He found himself staring at the holes in his sock while his boot remained happily on the floor. "Bootlaces," he said.

"Right," she agreed briskly, and began wading forward carefully, turning over what was movable and peeking beneath what was not. "Well, give me a hand!"

Without rising, he began poking about with a

perfectly good two-foot remnant of pole, complete with line and hook, which he fished from a nearby heap. The chance of finding any specific object in this great sea of stuff seemed remote. Then the hook caught on something deep in the pile and he played it like an angler, now tugging, now giving slack, now jerking at odd angles. Suddenly, it yielded and a blue tangle came flying into his lap. His first instinct was flight, but he was pretty well hemmed in. Then he realized his prize was just a clutter of woolen yarn, and he held it up to try to straighten it out.

"So that's where that went," she said, beaming.

"Is it some kind of fishnet?" he suggested, twisting it this way and that. He was startled when she seemed offended and tried to snatch it away from him. "Stop it! What's the matter with you?"

"It's not a fishnet, you dummy! I made it myself. It's a . . ." He was shocked to see her starting to cry. He didn't know what to say, so he looked closer at the thing he was holding. What was it? He tried to ignore the obvious eccentricities, rows of knitting that protruded oddly but confidently, only to be tied off and abandoned, threads waving limply like the pitifully beseeching tentacles of a beached sea creature. And he tried to ignore the unlikely yellowy-greeny shade of blue, something like the color of the sky if it had indigestion. He was left with a hemispherical object featuring peculiar extrusions that might be . . . earflaps!

"It's a hat!" he exclaimed and promptly pulled it over his head.

She laughed through her tears at that. "Silly, you've got it on backward." She waded over to him and began to adjust the various angles. "At least I thought it was backward," she mumbled, beginning to look teary again.

"Never mind," he reassured her, "it's the sort of hat that can be worn a number of ways. I like it. You say you made it yourself?"

"Yes, I was making it for my husband. It's not really finished. I was trying to surprise him. You see, I was taught to make fine needlepoints and embroideries and things that weren't much use in a cave or a cottage, so I was teaching myself to knit as a surprise for him, when he . . ." She gestured with her hand. "You know."

"How did he die?" the man asked very seriously, which he would not have been able to do if he could have seen how he looked in the hat.

"It was a . . ." She sniffed a bit. "A dairy accident."

"Dairy accident?"

"He was trod upon by the cow. You see, as he got older, he thought more and more about the days when he was young. We were always happy together, first in our cave and later on our farm, but he got to thinking more and more about when he had no responsibilities, when the world seemed a simpler place.

"One day, he told some of the neighbors' kids about how he'd killed a dragon when he wasn't much older than they were. Of course they didn't believe him, so he tried to show how he did it. He cut a reed, which he called a sword, and crept them up to the door of the barn, which he said was the dragon's cave. Then he gave a yell and did a double roll right under poor Esmerelda, our milk cow. And if she'd been a dragon and that reed had been a sword, she'd have been slain for sure. But she was just a cow and a skittish one, too, and she leaped right straight up into the air. Unfortunately, there was nothing in my husband's training about getting out of the way of slain dragons on their way back down.

"So I put him on a cart and took him up the mountain to bury him beside the old dragon, who had taught him a lot of new truths but hadn't cured him of nostalgia for the old lies. And when I got back, I tossed that hat in someplace else. You can keep it if you like."

"Thank you," he said, seeing no alternative.

As she continued her search, he stood and caught a glimpse of himself in a mirror. He threw up a startled hand to touch the contraption on his head and turned away. It took a moment to realize that his reflection had thrown up the wrong hand. He looked back and saw it wasn't a mirror, but a window. He shook his head and sat again. "I think I'm going crazy. Maybe I'd better just leave."

"Ha!" she exulted and darted into the quagmire a hand like a long-necked bird, coming up with two long stringy things that she dangled proudly in front of him like worms for a hungry chick. "Boot-laces!" she proclaimed, then looked at them closer. "There's nothing wrong with them. How'd they get in there?" She shrugged and dropped them in his lap.

He slipped them quickly through the eyelets, looped them around his calves and tied them with swift movements. He stood up and stamped a bit. "Perfect. Now if I can just keep away from a certain well-laced side of bacon . . ."

She smiled. He smiled. There was a silence.

"Well," he said, "I guess there's nothing else to keep me, so . . ."

She shook her feet free of her domestic high tide and ushered him through the hall and onto the porch. Iggy was at the foot of the steps. He stared at the man's boots and a bit of drool appeared at the corners of his smile.

She stepped forward quickly. "Don't worry, I'll hold on to him until you're . . . So where's your wife now?" She blushed when she realized the words had slipped out. "I'm sorry, you certainly don't have to answer that."

"I know," he replied, "but you answered my questions and now it's time to finish the survey.

"One day a prince showed up at our cottage. He told of how he had set out years before to waken the girl who slept in the glass coffin. But on the way he saw a girl in a high tower. He particularly noticed her hair, because it was the color of gold and because it reached approximately seventy-eight feet to the ground. For some reason it seemed logical to him to grab hold and climb up. Twenty-five years had passed before he admitted to himself that exceedingly (not to say ridiculously) healthy hair did not constitute a valid basis for a mature relationship. He fled and came to our cottage to fulfill his original plan."

"He said this in front of you?"

"Yes. I would have been very offended if I hadn't understood exactly how he felt. Besides, I was sure of my wife's affections, so I let him stay."

"What was the first hint of trouble?"

"Probably the speed with which she packed her bags. I notice subtle things like that."

"And when she left, you came here?"

"Curiously, no. Suddenly all the things that had become tiresome to me seemed strangely precious. The cottage, the woods. I tried to cook breakfast for the little men, but my griddle cakes made them *all* grumpy and then you couldn't tell them apart. I tried to dance and sing with the birds and the animals, but they expressed their disapproval in cute little animal ways that required me to brush up on my laundry skills.

"Everyone left me there alone eventually. I moped around for a while and tried to keep things as they were, but it was hopeless. Finally, I pulled myself together and set out to find my destiny. And that brought me to the high point of my whole career, wallowing in the muck with a good judge of character." He nodded to Iggy, who snorted his approval and pulled against her restraining hand.

She shook her head. "Why do men and women insist on going back and making the one mistake they managed to miss in the first place?"

He looked surprised. "You think both paths were equally wrong?"

"Or equally right. There's not a great difference. The important thing is to make a choice and live with it. You can make good or bad out of anything if you just stick with it."

After a moment, he nodded and smiled a bit. "Perhaps you're right. Now, if you'll excuse me . . ."

"And your name? Just for our records."

He grimaced. "Charming. It was my mother's idea, not mine, I assure you." He slid carefully past Iggy, who groveled at his feet, and headed for the gate.

"Isn't there still a question to be answered?" she called. He looked at her inquiringly. "What would happen if you kissed me now?"

He leaned against the fence. "I've thought about that. You might fall instantly in love with me. Or you might not. There's really no way to say for sure."

"Well," she said, scratching behind the pig's ears, "there is one way." And she closed her eyes and turned her face up toward him.

With a great sense of disbelief, he crept close. Her face still tilted upward. Even with her eyes closed, he could remember their deep green. And the few lines and wrinkles did not mar the alabaster of her skin or the black arch of her brows.

He bent and pressed his lips to hers.

Instantly she fell to the ground in a deep sleep.

"Oh, no!" he shouted. "What have I done? I've reversed the spell somehow! She'll sleep for another hundred years! What do I do now?"

She stood up then and kissed him on the cheek. "You'll have to get used to that," she said. "I have almost no housecleaning skills, but I do have a terrific sense of humor."

He felt weak at the knees, yet exhilarated. He tried to speak and made a sort of clucking noise.

She ignored him and continued in a businesslike but not unfriendly manner. "There's an empty house just down the road. You can stay there. We'll see what happens. All right? Charming?"

He laughed and shrugged. "Do I have a choice?"

She was very serious then. "You always have a choice. I like your hat."

He had forgotten the hat. It appeared that he was stuck with it. But just now, he didn't mind that or anything else in the world. He took a silent step toward her. He felt mud squoosh up between his toes.

"Iggy?" he asked, and looked around to see the porker chewing gaily on his second serving of laces for the day.

She shrugged. "You have to keep a tight grip on things around here."

He shook his head. "No, whatever you lose, you always have a chance to find it again in someplace else."

He smiled. She smiled.

They smiled.

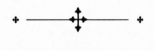

*And they smiled.*

She smiled. He smiled.

His smile faded first. Hers stayed frozen but began to crack.

He cleared his throat. She looked around nervously.

He started to speak, but she shushed him.

More time passed. The pig got bored and wandered off to shut itself in its pen and take a nap.

Finally he threw up his hands in frustration. "What's going on here?"

"Shh!" she cautioned. "Be patient. I'm sure we'll get a 'happily ever after' any sentence now. Just keep smiling."

After more nothing, she added, "Or at least a 'The End.'"

"This is ridiculous!" he fumed. "Our story is finished. Why are we still here?"

"Maybe something else is supposed to happen."

"Like what?"

"Like . . . I don't know, perhaps we talk some more and I fix you some dinner . . ."

"Sounds exciting."

". . . only the pig eats it!"

"A surprise ending! I can't wait!"

"It was just an idea. Anything could happen."

"Look, we talked, we worked things out, we tentatively got together, and we smiled. The End. This hanging around with no purpose is like . . . real life. It's unfit for any self-respecting fiction."

The sound of singing drifted up the lane.

"See!" she hissed in an undertone. "Something's happening. Oh," she exclaimed out loud, rather overacting, "who can that be now?"

"Who cares?" he muttered.

"Shh," she squeezed between her teeth as she smiled toward the front gate. The singing became clear as the voices of two children, a boy and a girl.

They danced into view after a moment and stopped.

"Look, Gretel," said the little boy, blond and rosy, dressed in lederhosen and alpine hat, "a gingerbread house, all covered with marzipan and candy!" The man and woman turned to look in bewilderment at the rough wood and shingle of the cottage.

"Oh, yes, Hansel," exclaimed the little girl, bright-eyed and pretty in dirndl and pigtails. "It looks good enough to eat! Yum, yum!" Her smile remained frozen as she finished in an undertone, "We've got the wrong house!"

"No," he whispered back, giving her arm a pinch, "I followed the directions precisely."

"Well, where's the candy?" she whined, rubbing her arm. "Where's the gingerbread? If I try to bite that thing, I'll need major dental work! And who are the grinning dummies with the wrinkly faces?" The adults came closer to hear what was being said.

"Please, ma'am," said Hansel, trying to get back in character, "we were out picking strawberries in the forest when we got lost, and . . . if you're the witch, who's your friend here?"

"Witch!" The Prince was indignant, although Aurora tried to calm him. "Who are you calling a witch, you little squirt?"

"Look, there's some kind of scheduling problem here. We're supposed to be doing a clever variation on the Hansel and Gretel story about two cute but obnoxious kids who eat the nice witch out of house and home so she finally has to bribe their parents to take them back."

"'Handful and Dreadful,'" the little girl chipped in. "That's the name of it. It's supposed to bring the book to an upbeat, amusing conclusion. It sounds like a blatant ripoff of O. Henry's 'Ransom of Red Chief' story if you ask me."

"But nobody asked you," Hansel whined, sticking out his tongue. Gretel crossed her eyes at him. For a moment they made faces at each other, seeing who could look the ugliest. They both won.

"So who are *you*?" asked Hansel of the grown-ups.

"Well, I'm Prince Charming and this is Princess Aurora, the Sleeping Beauty."

Gretel looked them up and down. "A little old for the parts, aren't you?"

"It's twenty-five years later," he explained. "It's a sort of middle-aged-regret kind of thing."

"Right," commented Gretel, stifling a yawn. "Nice hat."

Charming looked questioningly at Aurora. She gestured to his head and he reached up to touch the blue woolen thing that he had forgotten.

"I'm very fond of it," he said defensively, which made her smile.

"Uh-huh," said Hansel. "Whatever you say. Anyway, you're supposed to be out of here by now."

"Believe me," the woman assured him, "we'd like nothing better than to finish up, but we seem to be stuck here."

"How can you be stuck?" Hansel whined, stamping his foot. "You finish your story, you get your 'Happily ever after,' and you clear out before the next 'Once upon.' That's the way the Author works."

"Yeah, well," the Prince snapped back, "it looks like the Author is asleep at the switch this time."

The children blanched at that. "Don't say that," gasped Gretel. "You shouldn't even think things like that."

"Watch this," replied the Prince. He turned to Aurora. "I love you," he said, and kissed her. He looked at her expectantly.

"I'm not yet sure how I feel about you," she said uncomfortably.

He rolled his eyes and whispered, "Just go along with me for a minute, all right?"

She sighed. "I love you," she said unconvincingly, and kissed him quickly.

They looked into each other's eyes.

He smiled. She smiled. Sort of.

They smiled.

"**S**o *do you see any sign* of a happy ending?" the Prince demanded.

"Not an 'ever after' in sight," Hansel had to agree.

"I think that's just not the end yet," the Princess offered.

"What could follow that?" asked Hansel. "It was definitely an ending. I wouldn't call it very well written, but it was definitely—"

A bolt of lightning shot out of the blue sky and incinerated Hansel where he stood.

"I liked it!" Gretel shouted. "It was very well written! Real style and punch and—" The rest of her sentence was drowned by the roar of the tornado funnel, which plucked her like an apple and carried her off.

In an instant the scene was again all peace and quiet and gentle birdsong.

"What's happening?" Aurora gasped, afraid to break the silence. "Why is the Author doing this?" She took a step toward the Prince, but he gestured her away.

"I think I'm next," he said, looking skyward. "You'd better stand back."

"Why do you say that?"

"It's just a feeling I have," he said as the meteorite crashed to earth, then bounded away, leaving only a crater where he had been standing.

She was horrified and looked down into the crater, fearful of what she would see, but there was nothing left of him. He had been smashed to bits.

She drew herself together and looked up into the sky then, waiting for her own doom. Her chin trembled for a moment, but she lifted it higher and held it firm.

"You look exquisite like that!" called a voice.

She looked around, startled, and saw a young man leaning on the gate. "You'd better not linger," she said. "This seems to be a very unlucky neighborhood just now."

He laughed. "I'm not worried. And you shouldn't

be, either. Nothing could possibly happen to such beauty."

She looked at him more closely. He was young, tall, and exceedingly handsome, with golden hair spilling onto broad shoulders. She thought a moment of the unfortunate Prince, who had just been the victim of an unlikely interplanetary conjunction, but she couldn't even remember his name as she gazed at the handsome youth.

"Who are you?" she gasped.

"An admirer." He smiled and flashed teeth of such dazzling whiteness that her breath caught in her throat. "I have come to take you away from all this."

"To where?"

"To the place where dreams are true." He gestured, and she turned to see the gleaming white castle that soared where her cottage had squatted a moment before.

"Oh," she breathed, "it is so beautiful! I have dreamed of such a place."

"And now it is yours," he whispered, stepping close behind her and placing his strong, youthful hands on her shoulders. "And mine."

She turned slowly to him. "It seems that I have

been asleep all my life, not just the hundred years allotted. Now I awaken and am blinded by my first sight. But I shall never need to see anything again, so long as I can remember this first glimpse of you."

"Do you love me?"

She spoke not a word but folded herself into his embrace to give answer with a kiss. He took her up in his arms and carried her across the moat, blue water and blue sky reflecting in the even more glorious blue of his eyes, as they entered into the place of dreams.

And they lived happily ever af

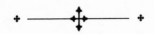

"*Blue!" she remembered* in a shout. "His hat was blue and ridiculous, but he wore it for me and perhaps I loved him, whatever his name was. Put me down!" And she kicked her legs until the young man had to set her back down. She looked around to be sure her muddy yard and cottage were back in their proper places.

"Good!" she stated. "Let's keep it this way. Now you just stand over there and answer some questions. Who are you and why was I acting that way and talking like I never did in my life? 'Blinded by my first sight' indeed! And where do you get your magic tricks, and do you happen to have anything to do with the recent high incidence of unusually localized meteorological phenomena?"

The young man looked sheepish and glanced thoughtfully for a moment at the gate, as if considering flight. Finally, he said timidly, "I'm the author."

✛    ✛    ✛

*For a while there was nothing.* Blackness.

Her hair was almost black.

Then there was whiteness.

A memory of the sublime paleness of her face.

That led him to the bright flash of her eyes. Strange, he couldn't conjure their emerald green, only shades of gray, but he was reminded that he had eyes of his own, which he opened.

Black and white.

Bright flashes against total void. The absoluteness of the view made it almost unseeable.

He finally made out a small white shape and spoke to it.

"Excuse me."

"Yes."

"Can you tell me where I am?"

"Yes."

"Well? Where am I?"

"Yes."

"Is that all you can say?"

The figure suddenly turned black. "No," it said.

"Good." He was a little startled, but determined to proceed. "Then would you mind telling me where I am?"

"No."

"No you won't tell me, or no you wouldn't mind?"

The black figure replied, "No." Then it flipped to white and said, "Yes."

"Stop a bit!" he called as the shape began to drift away.

"No point in stopping a bit," came a voice, "not if you want any answers besides 'yes' and 'no.'" He turned to confront a strange, squirming figure in shades of gray. "A bit can't even give you the time of day. It's all day or night with them. What you need is a byte."

"I'm lost, not hungry."

The figure laughed in many different voices and he realized then that it was not a single gray figure, but eight of the black and white bits clinging together. First one would be the head and spokesperson, then another would squirm up to take its place. And they changed from black to white and back again as they moved in ever-changing combinations.

Watching this made him feel a little queasy. "Do you know what has happened to me?"

"Perhaps," it replied, obviously pleased with itself.

"I'm not sure that's any more helpful."

"Of course it is. A bit is only a positive or negative electronic charge, plus or minus, so it can only tell you yes or no. When eight bits join together in a byte, such as yours truly, there are 256 possible combinations of yeses and noes. This makes for a really splendid range of ambiguity."

"But I'm looking for some certainty," he said impatiently. "What happened to me?"

"You were smashed to bits."

"Is this another pun?"

"Yes, but it's also simple truth. The two are not mutually exclusive, you know. The meteorite reduced you to your component electronic impulses. Look at yourself!"

He looked down at himself and saw the flashing blacks and whites. That body he had been used to, if not happy with, had lost all its mixed emotions and was now a swirling cloud of pluses and minuses, yeses and noes.

"You are located in the hard disk drive of the author's computer, specifically in the section where his WordPerfect program resides. You are currently disorganized, but eventually he'll restructure all your impulses as another character and then you'll show up in another story."

"No!" he insisted as a wave of remembrance washed over him. "I have to get back, and as myself. She's alone there. Aurora, my princess. We had just found happiness. Perhaps. I can't leave her alone. I love her! Can you tell me where she is?"

"Sure. She's on this disk, spinning along at hundreds of revolutions per second just as you are. Exactly *where* on the disk is more problematic. But she's not alone. The author wrote himself into the story and is with her now."

He tried to step forward, but the cloud that was him just churned in place. "The Author? There really is an Author? What is he doing with . . . ? I have to get back to her!"

"You'll just have to wait until the author rewrites you, and then of course you won't remember anything about her, so you might as well relax and accept it. We, for instance, were the second 'o' in the tornado the author was going to use to dispose of you, but he decided that was repetitive, so he changed it to a meteorite. Since 'meteorite' has only one 'o,' we were flushed into the bit pool and have been roaming since then, seeing the sights and waiting to be used again."

The cloud that had been the Prince was appalled. "You just let him run your life, make every decision for you? Well, not me." He gathered up his resolve. "If this author can do it, so can I." And he began to remember himself.

For a moment, nothing happened, but the thought of her and his years of yearning for her became a glowing heart at the center of his galaxy, and the pluses and minuses began to come together in configurations. "Yes" wrestled with "no" until both collapsed in a giddy heap of "maybe." Perhaps became possibility. Gray tones began to appear, then hints of color, then form and shape.

He thought of all the ways he could be improved, then decided that he must work with what he had been given. He selected among possibilities, rejecting with a sigh what might have been for what in fact *had* been.

With a great effort of will, he pulled himself to-gether.

Finally, he floated there whole, Prince Charming as he had been, for better or worse. He took a deep breath and swam off into the void to find her, how-ever hard the disk might be.

The byte went completely white in admiration of the Prince's resolution. The thought of the author's arbitrary despotism and irritating prose style black-ened its mood. It decided not to wait the author's bidding but to drift along in the Prince's wake and see what would happen.

"Nice hat," it called after him, putting on its gray shades.

+ + +

"*You're the Author?*"

The handsome young man smiled, shyly. "Yes, this is all my creation." He gestured around proudly, then realized he was pointing at nothing but rough wood and mud. He was embarrassed again. "And, of course . . . you." He blushed.

"Me."

"Yes. I created you. You are my favorite. All the others became tiresome, so I got rid of them."

"You killed them."

"I wouldn't put it that way. It wasn't really 'killing' them. They were just figments of my imagination, after all."

"Like me."

"No, you're different."

"In what way am I different? What's to protect me from becoming tiresome and getting your standard figment treatment?" demanded Aurora.

He was blushing again. "You're different, and you're safe because I love you."

✢   ✢   ✢

*H*e *was beginning* to feel his old self and more than a little angry as he strode through the wasteland, kicking aside flashing bits of information that swirled about his ankles like phosphorescent foam in the waves of a night sea.

Ahead of him, an area of color and motion showed unclearly through the electronic shimmer of rejected bytes hovering around it. He moved close to its surface and, after a hesitation, thrust his head through into the scene.

He saw a balcony. A King and Queen. A cheer seemed to be starting, so he shouted, "Huzzah!"

into what was suddenly a dead silence. The King threw a vicious look toward him and he pulled back into the void. Wrong story.

More wasteland. Then, a little farther on, he stepped through into a splendid room where a woman and a man sat at a table on which a single rose floated in a bowl. He saw only the man's back and wondered for a moment if this was the author, but the woman's face turned toward his and it was both pitifully ugly and filled with horror at the sight of him. Not his Princess. He stepped back quickly out of the story and proceeded.

The byte was still following him. "You're going to need some help if you're going to face the author," it called.

"Talk to me as we walk," returned the Prince, never slowing.

⁜　⁜　⁜

"*Of course I'm not really here.* I'm just writing a representation of myself into the story so that I can talk to you directly. So I can tell you that I . . ."

"Love me? Love me!" Her green eyes flashed with wrath and she tossed back her almost-black hair from the alabaster of her face, like a night-sea wave curling with phosphorescent foam. . . .

"Stop it! Stop describing me like that! I don't want to be beautiful when I'm angry, I just want to be angry."

"Sorry."

She was very angry.

"That's better." What could she do? Keep him talking, she decided. Maybe there was a way out of this. "All right, you wanted to talk to me. Talk."

"About what?"

"What do authors talk about? I don't know, where do you get your ideas?"

"Well, my plots are drawn mainly from traditional stories . . ."

"Stolen, in other words. But I don't really care about your plots. Where do you get your characters?"

"Well, they're all . . . that is, *you're* all drawn from my personal experience, people I've known, that sort of thing."

"So I was . . . ?"

The author smiled. "You. You were a girl . . . a woman, I should say, for whom I cared very much. She was beautiful, of course, but I loved her more

for her intelligence, her independence of thought."
He grew animated as he spoke, and Aurora was reminded of someone.

"So you love me for my fierce, independent spirit, and to prove it you try to write me into something else so I'll placidly toddle off with you."

He grinned sheepishly. "I didn't do very well with her, either."

"I assumed as much, since you've been reduced to dating fictional characters."

His faint smile was rueful. "You're all that I have left of her. But you're better than she was because you're consistent, you're comprehensible. I understand what you do. You're not capricious."

"You mean I do what you want me to."

"But you don't! You've surprised me again and again. Just when I think I know you, you do something I never could have written for you. I began to think that you were my big chance, the one really meant for me."

"Charming!" she blurted.

"Thank you," he answered uncertainly.

"No, that was his name and that's who you remind me of, Prince Charming. He had that same woebegone look and the same talk of being down to his last chance. But it's silly for *you*, since you're young and handsome. Or at least this representation is." She looked at him shrewdly. "What do you really look like?"

He looked away. "A little older, a little plainer. Thinner on top and thicker in the middle. A lot like Charming, in fact. He was . . . my first attempt to meet you."

"You mean he was you? Then how could you bear to kill him off?"

"I realized he was all the things I hate in myself: weakness, indecision, uncertainty. And I was jealous of him for the time he spent with you."

"I liked him," she mused. "He had his problems, but he was sincere and earnest and funny, too. And he wore my hat."

"But he didn't like it!"

"Of course not. It was ugly. He hated it but wore it anyway. For me."

"Well, that's all very well, but he's gone now and that's that."

"Couldn't you bring him back?"

"That would violate all the rules I write by. He died quite definitively and I can't change my own rules."

"You could."

"Not and live with myself."

"But you *could.*"

"Enough of that!" There was a cold glint in his eye. "It's time to discuss what *I* want."

✢   ✢   ✢

*A muddy yard. Her* muddy yard! He rushed across it and peered in the window. There she was! Bent over, searching. His heart leaped at the sight. Suddenly his own face rose and looked at him through the window. He on the porch threw a startled hand to his head, even as he in the room did the same with the opposite hand. He ducked away and out of the scene.

He was one story too early. But he was getting close.

✢   ✢   ✢

*She took a quick step* back. "Stay away or . . ."

"Or what?" he asked politely, moving toward her.

She grabbed up a rock to strike with. But it became a sponge in her hand. She ran, but the mud slid beneath her feet and, dreamlike, she ran without moving from her place.

He put his strong hand on her shoulder. "I created you," he said. "You're mine."

"But you shan't have her!" shouted the voice of Prince Charming. Aurora cried out with joy as she saw the blue hat first, atop a shimmering cloud, then the rest of him quickly materializing. She ran into his arms as soon as they appeared.

"How did you . . . ?" The author couldn't even frame his question.

"I had a bit of help." The Prince smiled.

"You'll need more than that," the author barked.

Suddenly, with a terrible roar, a tornad swooped down on the Prince.

"A what?" asked the Princess.

"A 'tornad,'" replied the Prince, laughing and brushing the meaningless letters out of his way. "That's what you get when your byte is averse to your bark."

He spoke firmly to the author, who was spluttering in rage. "Listen, you, before you try anything else, I've been taking a little tour of your computer. I visited each of your stories, and I . . ."

"You what!"

✳ 🦌 ✳ ❨ 🐿

*𝒯he author begins to strike* furiously at the computer keyboard.

Punch Shift, Function Key 3, "Switch Screens." The Document 2 screen comes up blank. Shift F10, "Document to be Retrieved: Untold." It appears. F2, "Search" for the phrase "Blue hat." A moment's whirring, then . . .

He's there! In all the stories!

Hit Shift F3. "Switch" back to Document 1.

✳ 🦌 ✳ ❨ 🐿

"*𝓗ow could you* do that?" the author moaned. "I'll have to read and correct it all again to be sure you haven't . . . Wait a minute. What were those symbols?"

"I got tired of those dingbats you use to indicate scene changes," said the Prince in the blue hat, "so I changed them. Anyway, the point is that there's been a basic shift in the power structure hereabouts."

"Just because you've inconvenienced me somewhat doesn't mean I have to put up with—"

"Actually, it's more than a question of inconvenience. One of the things I discovered is that you're basically lazy." He held up his hands disarmingly. "Not to judge you—I'm rather lazy myself." The Princess gave the author a meaningful look at that, but he refused to return it.

"I discovered that you never Back Up your stories, you just Save them to the Hard Disk. Forgive me if I'm a little stiff with this terminology. Anyway, I learned that the only copy of your stories is what I blundered into. You've never printed them out, never Saved them on Floppy Disk. This raised interesting possibilities, and I discussed them with the second 'o' in your short-winded tornado. It helped me fix things. Now if you attempt to print, copy, or otherwise transmit the document named 'Untold,' which contains all your stories, it will disappear, as you meant me to do, into a great electronic jumble, which I for one would consider an improvement."

The young man gaped, speechless, for a moment. "You . . . you can't do that! I'm the author here!"

"Abuse of authorial privilege," Aurora suggested. "You can have your artistic license revoked."

"This is not a joke!" the author snapped. "It's serious!"

"Not like the trivial question of our survival."

"I know, I know, that's important to me too. I do feel some responsibility, you know. After all, I gave you both extra life. Where would you be now if I had let your story end where it was supposed to?"

She thought about that for a moment, and her eyes turned inward to depths the author could never imagine writing. "We would be Between the Stories. That is where we go to live happily ever after."

"Do you really think this place exists in fact?" the author asked, doubtfully.

She smiled serenely. "I am a fiction. What do I care for facts? It is what I believe."

"But I could always write another story about you."

"That would not be truly me. Like the story you wrote before, in your other book . . . I have the memories that you gave me, but she was not me. And the girl/woman from your world was not me, either."

The author tore his eyes away to look at the Prince, who was gazing at Aurora with an expression of mingled admiration and doubt that mirrored his own. "Do you believe in this Between the Stories?" the author asked quietly.

The Prince looked back at him, and there was sudden understanding in their shared gaze. "No, I think I've seen where we go. It's a harsh place full of dark and light, and gray is its only color. From bits we come, to bits return, and the story is just an interlude of color and motion.

"But we have the opportunity within that space to live a life of perfect shape and duration, the chance to persevere through our adventures to an instant of ultimate happiness and end with an apt phrase. Can *you* hope for as much?"

After a moment, the author sighed. "I'm sorry," he said quietly. "I was wrong. I did it for love, but I was wrong. I will leave you now."

He turned and started to walk slowly away.

"Wait!" the Prince called after him. "Your stories. I'll fix it." His head disappeared into electronic shimmer and spoke to the byte that hovered there. "Thanks for your help. I can handle it from here." He pulled back into the story.

The byte ran through all its shades of gray and decided to hang around for a while. Just in case.

"All taken care of," said the Prince to the author. "And good luck with your stories. They aren't really as bad as I made them out to be."

"Thank you," said the author, and he stepped forward impulsively to face the Prince, then stopped, embarrassed.

The Princess laughed. "Two of a kind," she said happily. She stepped forward and joined all three into an embrace. When they stepped apart, she looked around in surprise. "Where are we?"

They were high on a mountain slope with a view over a peaceful valley. "Oh, it's a nicer spot for leave taking," said the author, "and I know someone here who produces a very fine vintage. Before I end your story, we must share a toast." He stepped into a cave for a moment and returned with a large goblet of wine. "The wine maker is taking a nap. We won't bother her." He offered the goblet to the Prince.

Taking it, the Prince turned to the Princess. "Should not the lady drink first?"

"No," said the author, quickly, "it is you I have most wronged and must reconcile with first."

The Prince hesitated, then raised the cup to his lips. In that moment the Princess saw again the cold gleam in the author's eye and cried, "Don't drink!" but was too late.

The Prince staggered toward her, moving his lips soundlessly. She took the goblet from him and tried to catch him in her arms, but he dropped like a stone. He lay on the ground, moving his arms feebly, trying for a last sight of her with eyes that wouldn't focus.

"I couldn't help it," the author said quickly. "I couldn't let him have you. So if he dies within the story, if he doesn't get his 'happily ever after,' he can't go off Between the Stories with you. But don't be sad. If you liked him, you'll come to like me, we just didn't get started well, that's all. I'll never end our story, I'll just keep adding to this file, I'll make it a novel and . . ."

She knelt beside the Prince, and he feebly held her hand but couldn't speak or raise himself. She looked down into the goblet she still held. "What's in it?"

"It's a poison, produced by a sorceress I made up for one of my other stories. She's sleeping now but will be awakened a little later by a King seeking a favor."

"If we waken her now, can't she give us an antidote?"

"No, absolutely impossible. I wrote this potion to be foolproof. It's made from the poisonous secretions of frogs and . . ."

"Frogs aren't poisonous!"

"Well, some are, I think. Anyway, this is my story and these are my rules. These poisonous secretions protect frogs from all but their own kind, so they work on absolutely every other form of life, including fictional ones."

"How long?"

"Only a few minutes. Then we can start our new life together."

"Absolutely no remedy," she mused, gazing down at the Prince's dimming eyes.

"Absolutely," the author agreed, proudly.

"Good," she whispered, and thrust the goblet to her lips.

"No!" the author screamed, and shook the ground with an earthquake. She held grimly to the cup but the wine spilled out before she could drink and soaked instantly into the ground. The author cried out in triumph but was frozen by her glance of utmost scorn.

A few drops had fallen on the Prince. Aurora tenderly kissed the wine from Charming's face and fell beside him.

"What have I done?" cried the author. "I have betrayed my own creation!" And he raved in despair about what he might do, how he could rewrite, knowing it was all useless but hoping for a last look from those fading emerald eyes that would give him some way to live with himself.

She focused only on the Prince, trying to whisper "Wait for me" but making no sound. She could feel he was almost gone. She willed herself to follow him with haste, but the author's noise kept dragging her back. With the last of her strength, she hurled the goblet at the sound of his whimpering.

The author ducked and the goblet clattered into the cave.

The echoes jogged his memory. "Hold on!" he called to the dying pair, and excitement and hope suddenly mingled in his voice.

He grabbed up a rock, banged it against the mouth of the cave, and yelled, "Hey in there!" When sounds came from deep in the cave, he turned back to the Prince and Princess.

"There is a stream down that way, near a castle, where you can find friends. All you have to do is . . . No, I've interfered too much already. Try to forgive me. I love you . . . both of you. Good-bye." And he was gone.

For a moment there was only the stillness of imminent death, then a three-legged shadow loomed up in the mouth of the cave.

"Nice hat," it said, and turned back to resume its interrupted slumbers, pausing just long enough to gesture magically.

And the mountainside was empty, except for two frogs, one with deep-green eyes and one in a silly blue hat. They were both exhausted, but the concentration of froggishness, which a moment before had been taking their lives, now roused and invigorated them.

And as they set off to join the stream, they were delighted to discover together, in their new frog language, all the amphibious words for love.

THE END

The author slumped, staring at the screen, then sat up with sudden resolution. "I'll fix it," he thought. "I'll change everything! I'll make the Prince just like me! Except with more hair. Then Aurora will love me . . . I mean him . . . and it'll be the story it always should have been! First, though, I'd better save a copy to be sure nothing happens to it." He began to strike keys.

F7. "Exit."

"Save Document? (Y/N)" appeared on the screen.

He reached a forefinger toward the "Y" for "Yes."

The second "o" in "tornado" had been waiting for this. It changed itself into an "N" in a fraction of a second and appeared on the screen next to "Save Document?"

"N" for no.

The screen went blank. The author tried everything he could, but the story was gone, lost forever in the computer. He couldn't save them!

"All right. No panic. This may even be better. I'll just write them again from scratch."

He typed.

And they smiled.

She smiled. He smiled.

His smile faded first. Hers stayed frozen, but began to crack.

He cleared his throat. She looked around nervously.

He began to sing "We all live in a yellow submarine." She accompanied him on the tuba.

"Wait a minute," thought the author, "that's a Beatles song! I never used incorrect-time-period jokes before. And it's not funny anyway. What's wrong with me?"

He quickly deleted the last paragraph and typed again.

The Prince looked at her seriously. "Who's on first?" he inquired.

"That's right," she answered.

"No, what's the name of the first baseman?"

"No, What's on second base."

"No!" shouted the author, deleting the whole page and starting again.

And they smiled.

She smiled. He smiled.

A tornado swept in though the author's window and carried off his computer.

He sat for a moment in shock. This seemed frighteningly familiar. A terrible suspicion came over him. He looked around. He saw the white expanse of a page in a book. He saw the number 164 at the top of the page. He looked down at himself and saw only the black letters that made up the words "the author."

"Who's writing this?" he asked politely, trying to stay calm.

When there was no answer, he carefully walked the tightrope of words to the edge and peeked over onto the following page. He saw the end of the story and the end of the book. And it ended with Aurora and Charming.

He climbed down the neat ladderwork of words to the bottom of the page. He didn't have far to go.

Beyond the end of his particular tale there were not even dingbats, just empty page. The author spoke wistfully into the blankness.

"Don't I even get to end with 'happily ever after?'"

In a swirl of plus and minus, of yes and no, Charming and Aurora disappeared together onto the hard disk. Prince and Princess, frog and frog, blue hat and green eyes, all dissolved into each other bit by bit, to mingle and twirl, the brightest flashes upon the revolving electronic dance floor.

So went they together Between the Stories as their tale was untold.

And, while they could not be said to live, they went happily to their ever after.